The Emigrant an

Winner of the Eludia Award

Hidden River Arts offers the Eludia Award for a first book-length unpublished novel or collection of stories by a woman writer, age 40 or above. The Eludia Award provides $1000 and publication by Hidden River Publishing on its Sowilo Press imprint. The purpose of the prize is to support the many women writers who meet with delays and obstacles in discovering their creative selves.

Hidden River Arts is an interdisciplinary arts organization dedicated to supporting and celebrating the unserved artists among us, particularly those outside the artistic and academic mainstream.

ADVANCE PRAISE

"Justine Dymond's *The Emigrant and Other Stories* traverses a breathtaking span of time, geography and emotion with authority and insight. Her compelling characters—an unwelcome minister's wife in colonial New England, an American teacher at a French prison, wedding guests forced to confront the conduct of their countrymen during World War II—find themselves navigating precarious new worlds, worlds that the author imagines with vivid precision unequalled in contemporary fiction. This is a masterful collection from a gifted stylist who knows the plants of western Tennessee, the rants of eastern Ireland, and the mysteries of the human psyche that draw people to distant lands. *The Emigrant and Other Stories* is as masterful, convincing and deeply nuanced a debut collection as any in recent memory."

—Jacob M. Appel, author of *Einstein's Beach House*

The Emigrant

AND

Other Stories

JUSTINE DYMOND

SOWILO PRESS

Philadelphia   2021

The author is grateful to the editors of the publications below in which some of these stories first appeared:

The Massachusetts Review and *The 2007 O. Henry Prize Stories:* "Cherubs"
The Briar Cliff Review: "The Emigrant"
Pleiades: "Pickpocket"
Meat for Tea: The Valley Review: "Geography Lesson"

Cover photo by Ryan McGuire
Cover design by Lesley MacLean
Interior design and typography by P. M. Gordon Associates

Library of Congress Control Number: 2020930453
ISBN 978-0-9994915-5-3

SOWILO PRESS
An imprint of Hidden River Publishing
Philadelphia, Pennsylvania

for Louis

Contents

The Emigrant
and Other Stories

Cherbs

When the cook heard the American tanks and motor cars rumbling up the muddy road from the west, she ran out of the kitchen, through the courtyard and past the barn, waving her apron, surrendering in delight.

This is what Béatrice tells us. In this moment that she tells us, we fear revealing any pride—those *Americans*, those Americans not unlike us, except separated by fifty-some years.

We think, Americans saved this house, St. Urbain, a mansion really. Tall ceilings, long hallways of rooms, a stone veranda with dancing cherubs atop its posts. A stretch of lawn that tumbles down to a pond and woods beyond. An estate. We think, the Americans—yes, the Americans!—saved the grandmother, the cook, and the maid, who stayed throughout the German occupation, *la grandmère* who refused to leave the house, even when arrangements were made for all the children—Béatrice was nine at the time—to stay in Nancy. And the cook, forced to make meals for those stinking Germans—except the Austrian officer, always polite, always respectful of *la famille*—the cook now gloriously freed from her servitude to men who didn't even

understand wine, who ate *coq au vin* as though they were animals
thrown raw meat, with no appreciation for subtlety of sauce, the
impeccable timing that renders the flesh tender.

We hesitate to smile at this. We do anyway—we know it's not
us, *we* didn't personally save St. Urbain from the Germans, but
Béatrice speaks as though those American soldiers, marching up
the road, tired, hungry, scared, were our kin.

Béatrice says, The cook ran into the road, waving her apron
at the American soldiers. See, *Maman* knew the Germans were
gone. It had been a full night and into the next morning with no
sounds of boots stomping overhead or voices shouting down the
cellar stairs—those Germans voices that provoked shudders and
tears in the maid as she and *Maman* huddled in the cellar. The
silence was all they needed to know. The Germans had evacu-
ated. Something else was coming.

When the cook ran out into the road waving her makeshift
flag of surrender, the Americans shot at her.

This is what we feared—even if only in that smallest part of
our consciousness that says, don't get carried away, chauvinistic
pride is always easily deflated.

Béatrice laughs at this point in her story.

We laugh, too, but a different kind of laughter, the kind that
expresses embarrassment, horror, shame at our own sense—how-
ever hesitant—of national pride. The Americans shot at the cook!

Then Béatrice is abruptly interrupted in her story by one
of the cousin bridesmaids reminding her of something urgent,
something we can't quite make out, but something to do with the
banquet arrangements, musicians who need something, and Béatrice is whisked away, leaving us to absorb this shocking change
in events—the saviors, the Americans, who shoot at the cook.

Was she hurt? we wonder.

We look around us, at the cousins and uncles and aunts running around, preparing for the wedding, the reason everyone has

gathered for the weekend, for Claudine and Max's nuptials. And we consider—in our despair about a story cut short—should we stop one of the other aunts rushing by? Who's she? Isn't that Claudine's cousin Bette? Would she know what happened to the cook?

We have to know what happened to the cook, and not just out of curiosity, not just to know the ending. It's a matter of national pride, we say this jokingly, of course.

Well, there *is* the grandmother, Béatrice's *maman*, Claudine's *grandmère*, who is alive, who is here at the wedding, the matriarch of St. Urbain. She didn't die, wasn't shot by Americans. There is that. We must console ourselves with this thought for now, at least until Béatrice returns or we find someone else to finish the story for us.

Everyone looks busy now. Bette is arranging the flowers on the tables outside one of the parlors where there will be dancing after dinner. The other parlor, across the marble entranceway, is where *Grandmère* entertained *les américains* for coffee earlier that afternoon. She asked us polite questions. Where were we from? Did we like the goat cheese made in the local region? We sat on the edge of beautiful chairs, not elaborate, a bit worn actually, but nonetheless expressing a certain aristocratic class. We sipped the strong coffee as inconspicuously as possible. We smiled and wrapped our loose lips around pointed French words, inwardly grimacing at the sounds that emerged from our mouths.

The night before, Claudine's father, Jean-Paul, showed us the original Diderot encyclopedia owned by the family. Excitedly we watched as he took down a large volume from the bookcase in the parlor. Shouldn't it be kept in a temperature-regulated room? we thought, frowning, but not daring to say it aloud, remembering that we had to hide our gauche American ways, our obsession with the *right* way to do things, much like our obsessions with refrigeration, statistics, and showering.

Jean-Paul opened the encyclopedia and we flinched at the sound of the spine cracking. But we brushed this aside and oohed and aahed over the simplistic maps of Africa and America, the vast sweeps of earth Europeans thought of as savage lands, unpeopled, unsettled. We admired the columns of careful French cursive, the compiling of knowledge as though a thing of fragile beauty, vulnerable to thieves and natural disasters. We wanted to caress the pages with our hands, though we repressed this urge, and merely nodded in agreement to everything Jean-Paul said, even when we didn't understand.

We took all that knowledge to bed with us that night, tucked in with us in the narrow, sagging mattress, our room an old servant's *chambre* above the barn. It looked as though the room hadn't been occupied since World War Two, but that's okay, we tell each other, it was nice of Claudine's family to arrange accommodations. Maybe this is where the cook slept! Over the barn, planning the meals for German officers, grimacing at the thought of wasting precious hens and pigs and goats on the swine. Béatrice had said that the cook, though she could speak German—indeed, her father was German, refused to speak their language to the occupiers, forcing them to rely on the shaky French of one young assistant to the Commandant. But she understood everything they said, as she stirred soup in the kitchen, spitting and stirring, adding cod liver oil and rotting tomatoes. The next morning she watched from the dining room window, while she laid out bread and butter. The officers ran to the pine bushes lining the driveway. She cackled. She didn't care. Let them kill her, after they shit out their bowels. She'd be happy to die for poisoning Germans.

But the Germans didn't kill her. The *Americans* shot at the cook!

We wander toward the hallway, watch through the window as the caterer's helpers set up chairs and tables in the barn, where the reception will be held. There's a makeshift stage and flowers strewn along the tables. There are candles and white tablecloths. Earlier that morning we helped sweep the barn and the courtyard, move furniture and wash the windows—what they really needed was a new coat of paint. We did our part. We joined in and made ourselves useful. Now we feel a bit in the way, without a task, without purpose. Except to hear the end of the story. We head towards the stairway, hesitate a moment, hoping for a glance of Béatrice through the open kitchen door. We see an army of people chopping and stirring food, but no Béatrice.

Under the stairway is the door to *Grandmère*'s rooms. She is resting now, we've been told, saving her energy for the church ceremony. We climb the stairs, curving up and around to the second floor, a wide hallway with windows to one side, looking down on the courtyard, and rooms on the other side. We hear the murmur of activity behind the bride's door. We wish we could be there, to be one of the "chosen" to spend the few hours before the ceremony with the bride and groom, helping to pin dresses and rouge cheeks, to keep track of corsages and run the myriad last minute errands that always need doing.

But we are guests, we are *les américains*. We've been told to relax, to enjoy ourselves, to take advantage of the countryside and the early summer air. Instead, we turn at the top of the stairs and navigate the narrow hallway filled with bookcases and bric-a-brac and cross the wooden planks to our room. We decide to take a nap. We lie down, face-to-face, nose-to-nose, on the narrow mattress, huddling for warmth—it's chilly in the servants' quarters!—and smile, knowing we won't sleep, impossible to sleep with all the activity around us, knowing that a dozen people are working below us, and with the mattress so sagged, so bowed, that in minutes we are fidgety, our backs ache.

We are too soft, too accustomed to the comforts of the New World, too coddled. We laugh at our own fragility. How do the

French do it? How do they stay so focused on what matters—love, life, ideas—when their mattresses sag and their rooms are dusty? We are clearly weaker, inflexible, unable to adapt. We don't admit it, but we could die right now for wall-to-wall carpeting and big, fluffy pillows.

What did this room look like when the cook lived here? We imagine a small dresser with a shrine to the Virgin, the cook waking early before sunrise, lighting a candle and saying a short prayer. She would have worn solid, leather boots, the kind that laced up, and she probably only had two changes of clothes. She would have used the kitchen sink to wash her face and then brew coffee. She'd have to feed the animals on her own, take care of all the barnyard chores since the stablehands had left to join the Resistance.

Yes, the Resistance! The cook longed to join the Resistance, but she knew that she must stay to help the family. In a way, she was a part of the Resistance, she would think to herself. She prepared *le petit-déjeuner* for Madame and her maid, first. She knocked on the cellar door before clomping down the narrow stairs. She recounted to Madame what the Germans had been saying. They sound worried, she said. They say *Die Amerikaner* often. They seemed to always be studying maps, rolling them up quickly when she entered the parlor with bread and coffee (just a little dirt added).

We think of the grandmother, so petite and frail now, her delicate ways. But to think she refused to leave the house while the Germans were here. She was brave! She was young and so brave! What would we have done? And with seven children, finally taken to Nancy, arranged by the Austrian officer, the one who was very proper and correct with the children, the cook almost regretted having poisoned his soup too. But what could she do?

We are restless. We need to know what happened to the cook. And where is the maid now?

Though it's still a couple hours until the ceremony, we decide to dress. We've laid out our things, a dress, a pair of stockings, a once-pressed pair of pants, now a bit wrinkled from travel, a clean shirt. We dress, slowly, carefully, savoring the feel of clean, fancy clothes, the act of dressing, as though the entire day depended on it. We continue the story, reminding ourselves of what Béatrice has already said, trying to find a clue somewhere of what happened next.

The French had occupied the house before the Germans came. They were proper, very proper, with *la famille*. Most of the French officers camped in tents on the lawn, waking early to the sound of cows baying, udders engorged. The family confined themselves to the upper rooms and the kitchen, while the officers used the parlors for their headquarters. The family made a game of it, telling the youngest children that they were safe because the soldiers were with them.

When evacuation orders came, the commanding officer told Béatrice's father to leave, to get to Paris, to Nancy even. The Germans were coming. The father pleaded with *Maman*—now *Grandmère*—but she refused. It was her family's house after all, and she could not abandon it. She thought of the banquets and balls her parents had hosted, when she was just a little girl before the First World War. She thought of her own coming out on the eve of that war, the shells that fell in the garden, the east wing conservatory one morning imploded by a German bomber. The family didn't leave then. They slept in the cellar then, the family and the servants who stayed. How could she leave now?

And so the family waited. The French had left, clearing camp as carefully as possible, leaving behind only holes from their tent pegs in the lawn. The family waited. They went about their usual business. Then one day there was a peculiar silence in the countryside. The children were sent to the cellar where they huddled with Father. *Maman* sat in her parlor, very still, very patient, and waited. The cook got down on her knees and scrubbed the kitchen floor. Again. She wanted to have this to do, she couldn't bear the waiting. The maid wept in her room above the barn.

Maman sat, listening to the sound of the brush's bristles against the stone floor, and beyond that, silence. With dusk came the first growl of engines.

We stand in the narrow passage between our room and the main hall, telling ourselves this story. On the bookshelf is a hodge-podge of things—board games, tools, broken ceramic, and a helmet. We are shocked. We've passed by this bookshelf already a dozen times at least since the morning. Why hadn't we seen it before? It is heavy, smaller than we imagined a helmet to be—more like a cap. Its greenness reminds us of algae, of another war, of swamps. Inside in thick black ink: Johnson. An American name. We imagine a black American soldier, on his first tour of duty, his first time out of the U.S.—heck! his first time out of Georgia. A hero.

Except, we must remember, the Americans shot at the cook.

Someone is coming up the stairs. We hear footsteps and then gradually a head of short, black and gray hair appears. We can't believe our luck! It's Béatrice.

As she reaches the second floor, she sees us standing in the passageway with the helmet. We sort of gesture at her with it, a kind of wave with the helmet. We are saying, Look, here is proof, here is what war leaves behind, what stories leave behind.

Béatrice nods and smiles, showing us what she has in her hands, a bridesmaid's dress made of light green organza. She is delivering it to the room where the bride is sequestered. But Béatrice's nod promises us she will return.

We are delirious with anticipation. We turn the helmet over and over. We try it on, its heaviness pressing down on the skull like memory. Like history. We laugh at our own profundity. We are Americans after all. We are supposed to scoff at the shackles of history. We can slough off history like a snake sheds its skin, leave it behind for others to worry about.

And yet, here it is in our hands, solid, weighty, and green.

Béatrice gently takes the helmet from our hands, turns it over and says aloud, Johnson. We loved the American soldiers, she says. It meant coming back home with Father. It meant chocolate and chewing gum. We'd never had chewing gum before.

We think about chewing gum as though it were a brand new idea. We remember chewing it as children, swallowing countless lumps of gum hardened by endless chewing, and the fear that we would never digest it.

Yes, yes, we say, but what about the cook? What happened to her?

Béatrice flaps her hand and laughs. Oh, nothing. When the Americans were coming, they were scared and they shot at everything that moved. But once they got closer and saw it was just a lady with an apron, they stopped shooting.

We are certainly relieved—those scared American soldiers!— they didn't hurt the cook. But there is a small part of us that feels disappointed, the drama turned to comedy, to farce. Is it better that the Americans were scared, rather than fierce?

Why did this helmet get left behind?

That, I do not know, Béatrice says and turns, heads down the stairs.

We hastily replace the helmet and follow her, not wanting her to leave us once again in mid-story.

What happened to the maid and *Grandmère*? Did they stay with the Americans?

Oh, yes. And the children, we all came back with Father. The American soldiers taught us baseball. I think, actually, they were quite bored.

And with that Béatrice scurries into the kitchen, leaving us at the bottom of the stairs. We consider the kitchen, but now that we've dressed we don't want to risk spills and stains. We turn the other way and walk towards the veranda. The sunlight dapples the marble hallway and children burst suddenly from doors and around corners, chased by older cousins or frazzled mothers. We smile in our distraction, hoping we will be stopped and spoken to, but no one approaches and we pass through the hall and the doors to the veranda.

The veranda stretches across the front of the house. At its center, where we stand now, stairs lead to a gravel driveway and then to the lawn. Stone cherubs twist and frolic along the veranda railing, frozen in movement. We touch their faces, chipped and pockmarked by weather and wear, their stone skin warmed under the sun.

It's a beautiful day for a wedding, we say to each other and skip down the stairs, holding hands, feeling ourselves young again, like children, escaped from adult concerns and tasks. We run across the driveway, gravel flying out behind our shoes, and across the lawn, down down down to the edge of the pond.

Out of breath, we stop and turn around, look back at the mansion, now spread out against the sky like a patient etherized . . . yes, yes, we could be in an earlier era, when people drank champagne out of shoes and Americans flocked to Europe. If you squint your right eye, we say, to erase the car parked at the side of the house, it could be just as it was then. We could imagine buggies and horse-drawn carriages coming through the gates and across the driveway, stopping at the veranda stairs, discharging their well-heeled passengers for tea, for dinner, for a ball.

From where we stand on the lawn, hands, like a military salute, shielding our eyes from the sun, we see a flutter of movement behind a second-story window. The bride and her bridesmaids. The groom and his groomsmen. The preparations continue, time continues. We can look back, squinting into the sun, but what can we see, blinded, the story half-known, our desire, like children, fierce and fickle?

After the ceremony, we are driven back by a kind cousin and his wife. Scrunched in the back seat of the car, we listen to them exclaim about the wedding and we contribute what we can. Claudine was magnificent, so beautiful and serene, Max—Max in a tuxedo! What a laugh! Who would have guessed we'd ever see the day? And *Grandmère*, in the front pew of the church—the huge, austere church with its stone arches reaching so far above us that voices got lost and never returned from that spacious heaven. *Grandmère* so tiny and in her element. And the grandchildren— in costumes! they made their own costumes!—when they were called to the altar, they came marching like a parade of jesters and merry pranksters. Such formal elegance, such irreverent fun at the same time.

As we offer these observations and listen to the cousin and his wife, the car turns into the long private road, shaded by poplars, leading to St. Urbain. Up ahead we can see the stone gates, but not the house, so thick are the woods and so long is the road. It's as though we were approaching again for the first time. When we pass through the gates and St. Urbain appears close and large, we feel the coolness of the poplars' shade, and a surge in the stomach that can only be described as love. Everyone is silent in the car, only the crunch of rubber tires on gravel, and then, slowly, the faint, ethereal sound of a piano playing somewhere in the house.

Everyone gathers on the veranda stairs, with champagne flutes and snippets of food—bruschetta and stuffed mushrooms. We stand and chew, murmur things like, What a day! How beautiful they were! Do you remember when . . . ? We wait for the newly nuptialed to arrive, and after about an hour, as the sun starts to move further west, cutting a sharp line of shadow across the driveway, we hear the sounds of laughter and wheels coming through the gates.

They arrive in a horse-drawn carriage, and we exclaim at how it is exactly as we had imagined it in another era. Small children, children of cousins, are lifted up and into the carriage with the couple. Everyone wants a turn. Everyone wants to be like the bride and groom, at the center, at the focus of attention, or at least to be in the viewing range of such royalty.

Someone hands the bride and groom glasses of champagne while they are still in the carriage. The best man presents a toast. He is in a wheelchair that has to be lifted up and down the stone steps. He will tell us later that he was in a car accident, paralyzed from the waist down.

The toast said, we raise our glasses and sip our wine. From behind us there comes a sound like a wave crashing onto a rocky shore, and then fluttering whiteness bursts around our heads. First there are shrieks, and then laughter and murmurings, as the doves fly above us, bank and turn as a group, and then circle around the house out of sight.

The champagne tingles now inside our heads, and after the releasing of the doves, we are ready to witness anything. What's next? Will there be elephants and tap dancers? Acrobatics? Fire-eaters? We would be very impressed by sword swallowers, we agree. Yes, anything that involved ingesting fire or weaponry. Wouldn't it be great if more weddings were like circuses? Bride and groom would undergo intense trapeze training before declaring *I do* in the air. Now *that* would be devotion, not merely spectacle.

We follow the other guests as they follow the couple up the veranda stairs and through the house to the courtyard. We are going in for dinner. There will be more wine. There will be a long buffet table of food, deli meats displayed in the form of a peacock—yes, a peacock!—and cheeses and salads and, of course, long batons of bread, hard crusty baguettes that we will devour as though we have never eaten before. There are speeches and skits, singing, jokes, more speeches, voices slurred. And then, as we are imbibing another glass of wine—no use counting anymore, we lost count a while ago—we hear the strains of familiar music and a warm prickly sensation creeps up our backs, the body's knowledge, before the brain, that we are being watched. The music's familiarity wakes us from our gluttony before we consciously recognize the tune, and when we look up everyone is grinning at us. They are playing the Star Spangled Banner. Flushed with embarrassment, we grin back and then affect little waves, like Miss America on her float, acknowledging the loyalty of the masses.

It's not *spankled* banner. *Spangled* banner.

The couple next to us argues in English tinged with French vowels. And with that distraction comes relief. The music fades and everyone is invited back to the buffet table for fruit and more cheese and chocolate.

Outside the barn, it's now dark. We've been eating and drinking for hours. We feel properly medieval in our dedication to feasting. Guests are speaking and laughing louder, as they meander through the courtyard. Someone has started playing music in the house and candles are lit all along the walkway and into the house. But the air feels marvelously fresh and we linger outside, wobbling around the side of the barn.

We walk up to the road behind the barn, where the cook ran, waving her white apron. There is a tree just there, across the road, magnificently fat, its leaves rustling like a Victorian lady's underskirts. We turn toward the west. Fireflies blink across the dark. We can barely make out the reach of the road, we strain to see its horizon. The cook would have seen the soldiers coming, an indistinguishable mass of men, and then, here—we point to the tree, she would have fallen flat at the crack of gunfire. Would she

have yelled? Would she have called out, *Nous sommes les français!*
Or would she have lain still, just waiting, her heart pounding,
until the soldiers came so close that she could smell their sweat
and hear their breathing? She would have heard the harsh nasal
of an American soldier ordering her to stand up. And then once
on her feet, her apron flung forgotten on the ground, she would
have smiled and kissed the first soldier she saw. In her machine-
gun French, she would have scolded them for shooting at her
and taking so long to save them. The soldiers would relax, pull
out cigarettes and slump into the grass beside the road, thankful for a moment's rest. A lieutenant who studied French in high
school would be pushed forward to speak with the cook, and stu-
diously she would listen to his questions, his confusion of words,
his youthful fear as he asks, *Where are we?* Only, to the cook's
amusement, he is asking her, *Qui sommes-nous? Who are we?*

The cook would clap him on the shoulder and laugh, saying,
Mais, bien sûr, vous êtes les américains!

There is a sharp whistling sound and then a crack. We turn
pale—what is that? A moment of non-sound, as though the air
were sucked away, and then a fountain-spray of colorful light
beyond the house. We head back across the road and through the
courtyard. Everyone else is moving towards the house. More fireworks shoot off, one twirling and twisting like a snake, and then
crack crack crack as they explode above the house.

Guests crowd on the veranda, the bride and groom, too,
standing in the middle of the group like queen bees surrounded
by worker bees. We are all looking up, our necks stretched up
to the sky, its infinite backdrop. Our eyes reflect in miniature
the streams and bouquets and twinklings of fireworks. We are
hushed, we are awestruck, we are humbled by this god's display
of power.

It is like July 4th, is it not? Béatrice says. She is next to us,
looking up into the sky.

It is, we agree, but we don't want it to be. We want it instead to be like this, like a wedding, like champagne and chocolate, deli meats shaped into peacocks, cooks who refuse to speak German, *mamans* braving occupation, and the faces of each other in the light of sky.

Béatrice beckons us over to the far end of the veranda. She puts her hand on a stone cherub's head, her thumb tracing a concavity.

She speaks and we push closer, tilting our heads to hear her better.

Tu vois? You see these missing pieces? The American soldiers were so bored, she says. They had nothing to do all day but wait and wait.

We are stunned. We are speechless. Then there is a rush of popping and whistling, and the fireworks burst in a grand finale of noise and color. We look up and up and ooh and aah.

When we look down again, the guests are moving back into the house. There will be music and dancing well into the dawn, the bride and groom will slip quietly away to sleep, also the *grandmère* and her memories. Only the drunken few who deny the end of things will linger, clinging to each other, smiling wearily, picking at the ravaged buffet.

We won't want to give up either. And so we will stroll along the gravel driveway in the misty sunrise. Beside us, the bulletridden cheeks and arms and legs of the cherubs will stay frozen in their postures of flight, enduring beyond even this.

The Emigrant

The prison doors confuse me. I pass through dozens of them, without touching a single one, and down long hallways divided by bars and gates, corridors of cages. As I move deeper into the prison, I experience the sensation of moving away from, escaping from something, and I walk faster, trying to shake myself of this middle state, of passing through. When I'm done teaching for the day and the final, outer door closes behind me with a thud, air displaced by steel, I spread flat against the prison wall, feel my body fill in the craggy unevenness of stone.

To get to my apartment, I pass through a heavy iron lattice-work gate that takes more than a twist of the wrist to open. I have to lean my whole body into it, thrust a hip against it, push a shoulder at it, before it lets me in. In the lobby, my concierge's light brown face, her dark eyes, disappear behind a window curtain. And then there is another door. I often quiver and fumble with the key to the second door, its lightness and wood a surprising ease to open. It flies back against the wall, shudders in rebound. The curtain flickers again. I close the door slowly. I twist the knob back and then forth, letting the latch ease soundlessly into place.

Inside the apartment, doors circle the foyer: the front door, my bedroom, the bathroom, Richard's bedroom, the toilet closet, the kitchen. I must choose one of the doors. They are all closed, because that is the way the French live. And, as Richard reminds me nearly every day, *Doors are not kept open all the time here, like they are in America. If we want privacy, we lock our doors.*

Sometimes when I wake to pee in the middle of the night, I forget what country I'm in. I pause, swaying in my half-sleep, in front of the toilet closet that Richard and I share. I don't know whether to knock or not. So I scratch at the toilet door, just to be safe, and wait for the response of no response.

During the day, I hesitate in front of closed doors. If I knock, Richard scolds, *Entre l'americaine qui frappe.* If I don't knock, a part of me unconsciously slips, becomes unjoined, as when a sliding door comes off its track.

When he wants me, Richard barges in. Doors pose no obstacle to him. No confusion. No barrier.

I can't bring myself to lock my bedroom door, to slip the metal hook into its eye. I watch it dangle, unused, jiggling against the door when the apartment shakes under Richard's foot. I cannot lock him out, nor can I lock myself in. I listen carefully and watch the man who lives across the street. His apartment is at the same level and his desk faces the balcony window. He studies nearly every night. And I work with him, preparing grammar and pronunciation lessons. Drills on the objects in a room. Floor. Chair. Table. Window. Door. Lock. Bars. Guard.

The prison takes up a whole city block. In the wall is a red circle that buzzes when I press it. A guard opens the door and waits for me to flash him my I.D. I drop my watch, earrings, ring, and keys into a bowl that a guard holds out for me. He searches my bag, then looks at me with eyebrows raised as if to say, *That's all? You must have something else.*

He waves me through a security check, a square frame with a blinking red light. A loud alarm sounds. I wince—too much of Richard's gin last night. I step back then, surrender all the centimes and francs, their solid little bodies fatter than American coins, small enough to swallow one by one.

I think of Richard finding the gin bottle half empty, tucked back under the sink where he keeps it, next to dish detergent and bleach. Richard stashes it there for emergencies, which happen when he comes home after the stores close, some girl he found clinging to his arm. He doesn't even like gin. Someone gave him the gin for an occasion, Christmas, his birthday, Bastille Day. Richard probably doesn't remember himself. He's not very good at remembering. Most likely he cannot recall how I arrived at his apartment. A musician at Trois Maillots, a bar I went to my first week in Paris, knew Richard and knew that he had a room for rent. The night I showed up, Richard had 76, a God-awful French beer he served with endive salad and coq au vin. I admit he cooks well. He seduces well, too, but that's about all he does well. Sometimes when he sees me in the morning, he looks puzzled, as if his girl for the night had not taken the hint when he rolled over and said, *Eh bien, and tomorrow is another day, eh?* Eh bien, Richard only charges me 200 francs for the room. I also put up with Richard because of the way he says my name. The French pronounce Ariel as though it were chocolate melting on their tongues. I never appreciated my name until I came to Paris; the nasal American pronunciation constricted air rather than opened to the sky. Richard offers each syllable—Ahr-eee-elle—equally, and I feel myself swimming in his throat.

Finally clear of the security gate, I cross an inner courtyard. I keep my eye on the door ahead, a dark mouth in the inner prison wall. I focus on that darkness so that I do not see any new prisoners being led from police vans, hands cuffed, heads bent so the guards must guide them. I scurry through this courtyard, faster than the guards who strut or stroll, hands by their sides or fingers looped to belts, the sunlight dancing on their jangling keys. Hundreds of keys to hundreds of doors.

Inside the prison, I pass through a lobby where there is a booth, like an information kiosk at the train station. But there are no time schedules or maps or flyers. Just a guard, sitting at a consul of little screens and speaking into a microphone, a long stainless steel one that snakes out from the wall. The guard gives out information in short clips of sound. A woman talks hesitantly to the guard, her hand cupping the back of a small boy's head, her palm fitting perfectly to the slope at the base of his skull. The boy looks up, he is looking up at everything.

Once I cross the lobby, I wait for a guard to open an iron-barred gate, and then I enter another country. There are no female guards past this gate.

I catch myself looking down at my blouse to make sure it is securely buttoned. A drab olive-green cotton blouse. Black slacks. Clothes recommended by my supervisor, Hortense, who painted me a picture of lustful men, desperate to see females, ready to burst with deprivation. My clothes mask roundness and curve, give me shoulders instead of hips, a chest instead of breasts. But I am not fooling anyone.

When I first came here, I was surprised to see that the inmates wore street clothes and the guards wore gray or brown uniforms. I steeled myself for catcalls, lewd comments, and open staring. Long lines of prisoners waiting at intersections of barred gates made me grit my teeth, as though my clothes had melted away.

But nothing happened. Gates whined and clanked. Keys jangled. Men looked at me then away. I tried not to stare at them. Silence echoed down corridors of dank stone and iron bars. And I trembled with embarrassment, ashamed that I had expected reactions from these men, most of them North and Black African, who could not have cared less about a dumpy white girl in dull clothes.

Still I am anxious that I might slip: a button unbuttoned, pants too tight. Something that would blur the boundary between clothes and body. So I am stiff and awkward, walking without any extraneous movement or sound, I keep my hips centered and my butt tucked under my back, carrying my bag so it covers my chest. I inhale deeply, hold my breath, feel my heart pounding to get out.

I watch guards turn keys in locks and I whisper *Merci* when they hold the gates open for me. I train myself not to blink when the gates close behind me, when I pass the shower rooms, when I walk by the rows of prison cells, three stories high, each door solid steel with a peephole at eye level. I hear the thud and slap of cell doors opening and closing above me.

I climb a spiraling stone staircase, as fast as I can without running. At the top I walk another corridor, this one running east to west, at the end of which I ring a bell. M. Hardin, the education center guard, unlocks the door for me. *Bonjour, Mademoiselle,* he says, a sly smile creeping onto his face. He always has this smile. I want to know what the joke is. Am I the joke? Is the education center a joke? For me, the classroom, despite its iron latticework windows, is a small country of freedom, buried in the prison. It is what I brave all these doors for.

I wait for M. Hardin, who fumbles with the keys to the classroom. Students are arriving, packing into the corridor. They keep a polite distance from me as I look out the window. Below us in a courtyard, black heads circle inside an exercise cage. Someone brushes my arm—Khalil, a student, also watching the men below. *We are kept separate, you know,* he says without looking at me. He is unshaven and I can see individual black whiskers on his cheek and a small, whitish scar on his upper lip. *The black men and the brown men.* Then he turns to me and says, *They think we will start trouble if we're put together.*

Bon! M. Hardin swings open the door. I move quickly through the path the men make for me and into the classroom where I busy myself with my notes and look for chalk.

As the men shuffle in, they speak in Arabic to each other, all except Paul, the only Frenchman. He sits directly across the room from my desk, barely moving, looking straight ahead. I smile and nod at him. He nods back. After a few seconds, they all look at me, except Khalil who reads the dictionary. I feel like a conductor who is faking it, who doesn't even know how to read sheet music, surprised by the strange musical notes that come from the orchestra.

Khalil's hands are long and elegant, the bones distinct under mahogany skin. His fingers delicately turn a dictionary's pages, pinched between thumb and forefinger. His English is too good for him to be in this class. But it is one of those deliberate oversights M. Hardin shrugs his shoulders at. *Il n'y a rien qu'on puisse faire. There's nothing that can be done.*

But Khalil seems content enough to mine words—*gamb, gambit, gamble*—from the center's dictionary. The class is practicing the irregular past tense, repeating *I went, you went, she he went, you went, they went*, when Khalil raises his hand, the fingers relaxed and curled ever so slightly into his palm. These are hands that I imagine in fists, squeezing a neck or gripping a gun. I don't know why he's in prison. I do not ask.

Yes, Khalil?

This word, 'game,' he says.

Yes?

How do you use it?

The teacher in me, ready to make a lesson out of everything, looks around the room. *Who knows what 'game' means?*

Paul raises his hand.

Un jeu, he says.

Yes, but use it in a sentence.

I make a game of football.

Good. We say 'to play a game.' I play a game of football. Past tense?

I played a game of football.

Good. How else do we use 'game'?

The men stare back at me. They are waiting for me to give them the answer, so they can write it in their notebooks, memorize it in their cells, repeat it back to me tomorrow with pleasure in their voices. I like this, their hunger for words. It is while I'm poised there, hand in the air, noticing a shaft of sunlight creep up the back wall, dust particles floating in its bright swath, that I feel my blood stream into my limbs and my nerves tingle with energy. Khalil looks to be on the verge of an answer. My heart beats a little faster. I step away from my desk and walk inside the circle of tables they sit at.

A trick. Khalil.

Yes! I rush to the board and write 'trick.' *A sentence?*

Khalil gestures with his hand palm up, ready to receive.

I saw through his game. I write it on the board as I say it.

The men repeat after me, then scribble in their notebooks. All of them except Khalil. He doesn't have a notebook. He doesn't need one.

J'ai vu clair dans son jeu.

What else?

Silence. Pencils at full mast.

To be game to do something. To be willing. I write on the board, they write in their books. Khalil puts a hand on the dictionary as if to turn a page. But I don't want him to leave us yet, to burrow into his tunnel of words. *Khalil, are you game to learn English?*

Yes, he says, the corners of his mouth turned up. He looks at me from under a mass of unruly, thick, black hair. Sometimes his hand plows through this hair when he's thinking, when he's hunkered down with a slippery word. When he gets a joke. But now he is waiting for me to finish. He understands this word now; he no longer needs my assistance. He wants to return to the dictionary.

Now you make a sentence, I say.

He thinks a minute, plucks at the dictionary's pages. Then he asks, *Would you like to go to dinner?*

The men titter. They giggle. They understand.

I'm game, I say, grinning like a fool. He knows the word better than I do.

The thought of my room depresses me. The crates of clothes, the thin mattress on the floor, a rope strung up to hang dresses and coats on. Richard's smirking eyes.

After class, I wind my way up to Rue Mouffetard where the second hand clothes and hat shops are closing up. Clerks crank down metal doors and lock iron gates. I follow Rue Descartes to Place Maubert where I find a seat on a cafe patio, one of the few remaining seats which are quickly filling with the after-work crowd. My table is wedged between a couple smoking and talking intensely, punctuating words by jabbing their cigarettes in the air, and four young men, all wearing ties and speaking so fast that I can barely catch a familiar word.

A waiter approaches my table, points a hip in my direction but looks the other way. I order a kir, and the waiter is gone before the sound of my voice dissipates. Then I watch the cars swim around Place Maubert at the center of which a bronze man on a horse looks strangely out of place. The horse rears back, its front legs forever flailing over the whirl of traffic.

In the Latin Quarter I find a dark, crowded bar where I can squeeze into a corner and drink kirs all night long. There is an upright piano at which people take turns playing American show tunes. They pounce on the keys with incredible force, and the sound smacks my ears. With each song, the voices get louder and more off key, and I can't tell which voice is mine.

In front of my apartment building, I stand for a few minutes, feeling the ground surge and retreat under me. I gulp the air and glare at the front gate before tackling it. I think I see the concierge's curtain swing back and forth, but maybe I only imagine the movement. At the bottom of the stairs, I consider the elevator, a rickety wooden box with a folding door and a metal gate, but though the thought of three flights of stairs exhausts me, I decide against the vertical box.

From my room I can hear a female, that high airy soprano of so many French women, and then the front door shuts. My door opens and Richard, strands of black greasy hair dangling near his eyes, peers at me. I close my eyes quickly. *Ariel? Are you awake?* His voice gets closer until I open my eyes again and he is squatting right next to me. His gray robe hangs open: a pale, hairy body and white underwear.

So, who was it this time? I say.

Ah, ma petite Ariel. A nobody. She is not half as good as you. He rests a hand on my hip.

Nice try. But no thanks.

He stops caressing my hip and he stands up in one movement.

Putain, he says and leaves the room.

As I approach the spiral staircase, I can see Khalil being let out of his cell on the second floor. He wears sweat pants and flip flops, dragging his feet as he walks. I move fast up the stairs so that I arrive at the education center when Khalil does. I press the doorbell. Khalil says, *Bonjour Professor.*

Hello, Khalil. How are you?

He shrugs, then says, *You smell of the outside.*

How is that?

— 27 —

M. Hardin appears. *Allez, vite. Vite!* He waves us through, unlocks the classroom. Khalil steps back to let me enter.

You smell of cold.

I smile and bow my head, looking for chalk. The bell rings again and M. Hardin mutters as he goes to answer it. I look up to say something to Khalil but the dictionary is open and he's already digging for words.

I am full of what Khalil says to me as he leaves class. He returns the dictionary to my desk, sliding it towards me but keeping his hand flat on the cover. *Is it hard to emigrate to America?*

I hesitate, afraid of what my answer gives up of myself, my uncertainty and my fear. I worry about Khalil's next question.

Before I can decide what to answer, Khalil tells me that he will be released in a month. His sentence will be finished, and the prison will give him a ticket back to Morocco. He slides his hand back and forth on the dictionary as he tells me this.

I don't know, I say, still digesting what he said. I imagine his hands on my hips, my ass, my breasts. I blush.

He shrugs, and heads towards the door where M. Hardin waits. *A bientôt, Mademoiselle.* I leave, too, and return through the belly of the prison, to the outer wall, from which I am expelled back into Paris.

The sharp November light and the smells of this city overpower me after a morning in the dark mustiness of the prison. I notice for what seems the first time the lingering perfumes of other women who pass me on the sidewalk, the tinny odor of car exhaust, the meatiness of horse chestnuts roasting over a barrel fire by the metro station. All this reminds me how specific our pleasures are, how bound up they are in deprivation.

I feel fat with my own shame and disgust when I meet Hortense. I cannot eat. I push the salad and Camembert around on my plate, though Hortense insists that this is the best Camembert in the 14th arrondissement. She is a wiry woman who wears long, shapeless tops made of Indian prints and speaks English with a British accent. She is more fanatical about cheese than other French people.

I want to tell her what Khalil asked, ask her what I should have said. Instead, I say, *I'd like to bring in some audiotapes.*

Hortense glances at me quickly then concentrates on her soup again. *What for?*

So they can hear someone else speaking besides me.

Hortense gets a pained look on her face, then takes off her glasses and wipes them with a napkin. She puts them back on before saying, *Whatever you do, don't tell me about it.*

I stare at her, turning over this comment in my mind, while the waiter pours more wine for us.

You might think it odd, Hortense continues, as if she'd read my thoughts, *what I just remarked. It's not that I don't want to know what you do, but there are certain things, like audiotapes or books, that the guards don't like. Photocopies are okay.*

It's not against the rules, is it?

No, not strictly speaking. But guards are paranoid. I've tried to bring things in, and Hardin has taken them away. It's best if you just do it, and don't tell me. That way it is something you've done of your own free will.

For the rest of lunch Hortense explains where all the best cheese shops are. Gouda, Brie, Roquefort, brioches, baguettes, coffee, Beaujolais: it is a catalog of freedoms. She is cynical about the system and would probably tell me that my answer to Khalil—*I don't know*—was all I could give, that, if anything, it was too optimistic.

I sip a glass of cabernet and enjoy the warmth that trickles through me.

Back in the prison for my afternoon class, I am still light-headed from wine. To the students' obvious delight, I teach the advanced class all the swear words I know in English. They give me some in French. Salaud. Bastard. Con. Asshole. Connard. Jackass. Je te fous. Fuck you. Merde. Shit. Bordel de merde. A shit hole. Putain. Whore.

In the subways, the turnstiles are taller than I am, long sheets of steel with rubber flaps on the edges. I fear that they won't open or that they will close on me as I pass through. These kinds of turnstiles are only in the big stations, Place d'Italie, Champs-Élysées, L'Opéra, where there aren't enough police to patrol all the entrances. At Place d'Italie I see police with dogs chase an Arab and slam him up against a wall. He passed through a turnstile without paying. How he did it, I don't know. Maybe he was skinny enough to squeeze through the crack.

Richard comes home late that night and bangs around the kitchen cursing. Without knocking, he flings open my door. *Who drank my gin?* He waves the bottle.

Je ne sais pas. I shrug my shoulders. *Une de tes petites amies? One of your lady friends?*

He snorts and stumbles back into the hall. I hear a higher pitched voice, then a door slams and the voices are muffled.

The next morning, I wake to Khalil's voice in my head. *Is it hard to emigrate to America?*

I hardly remember anymore what I expected of Paris. Vaguely, I think of suave Frenchmen and days spent wandering *les jardins* and *les musées*. But now all that seems like another city, a different country. In college my French class watched a French language show that revolved around a buxom, blonde mademoiselle and her wealthy family. All her friends were white and sat in cafés while she hurried to school, to home, *aux jardins. Elle sort. Elle rentre. Elle voit. Elle entend. Ça ne va pas.*

The rain comes down in knives. Inside the prison, the men are restless. The exercise cages are empty. In class, Khalil doesn't look up from the dictionary, which I now put out on the table before he gets to class. My failure to give him an answer still hangs on me. I abandon my lesson plan, neatly arranged and outlined on lines of legal pad. Instead, I reach for anything to spark them. Said, a round and fatherly Senegalese, wears a World Cup t-shirt, so I get a few words from them about soccer, but their sudden energy flows into French and Arabic, and they become silent when I ask for English words. By noon, I want to crack my pounding head against the stone wall.

At the end of my final class of the day, M. Hardin appears in the doorway. Chairs scrape against the floor as the students get up to leave. I collect my things slowly, wait for the classroom to empty.

There is never enough air in here, I say as I pass M. Hardin.

Eh, bien, Respirez moins. He laughs as he opens the gate. It clangs shut behind me. When I look back through the bars, M. Hardin is still laughing at his own joke. *Well, then breathe less.*

Of course, I don't know what it's like to emigrate to America. I did have to get a work visa in Paris. Getting the visa was a hassle, but the ordeal was eased by my having a white face and an American passport.

On the far edge of southwest Paris, the immigration office is still technically within the city limits, but far enough from most immigrant communities to use up the better portion of a day. It took me an hour to get there by metro. Hortense had told me to go early in the morning, but even arriving at 8 a.m., I encountered a long line of people. When the doors finally opened, an official-looking man came out and asked us each what we were there for. Everyone else in line was either African or Asian. When the official got to me and I said a temporary work and residency visa, he waved me forward ahead of the others. I hesitated, and again he gestured impatiently. I scurried past the line of people, felt their haggard eyes following me.

An hour later I had been to several counters, had my photo taken, and was waiting on a cool marble bench for my visa to be assembled. When I got the card, freshly laminated, I caressed the smooth plastic still warm from the machine. I walked out of the building with a new page stamped and signed in my passport; the ink slightly smeared, the official seal cut off by the paper's edge. On my way out, I passed the river of faces, some of them the same ones I had seen an hour before, still waiting to get in.

On Saturday at Shakespeare & Co. I buy Khalil a used American Heritage with a hard, red cover and gold lettering on the front and spine. My hands tremble when I pay for it. I'm nervous. Do I look too obvious in a dress? Small black flowers and buttons up the front. A gift of words. What could possibly be wrong with that? I know that every word I speak in the prison is a cruel gift of hope. The students scribble the words down, impress me the next day with their ability to recall. But Khalil is not trying to impress anyone. He handles words not as gifts, eagerly, but the way a jeweler studies uncut stone, weighing the potential for brilliance and beauty, and for impurity.

Whatever you do, don't tell me about it. Putain.

A guard at the entrance asks me my purpose.

Je fais une visite, I say. *Visiting.*

At the security check a female guard opens my bag and pulls out the dictionary and my wallet.

Qu'est-ce que c'est?
A dictionary.
What for?
I'm an English teacher.

The guard wants more. She is waiting for my face to reveal something. Then she opens the book and shakes it by holding the front and back covers out like they are wings. She flips through the pages a couple times and peers down the opening between the spine and cover. Her performance is ridiculous, but I act nonchalant, look somewhere else, appear unconcerned. Then, just to be a nuisance, she opens my wallet and goes through all its pockets, taking out things I forgot were there. An old photo of me standing by Lake Erie, hands on hips, feet spread apart like a little kid. The water and sky a blue sheet. Then the guard pulls out my visa, an old credit card, my driver's license, some change and a 20 franc note. Not satisfied, she turns the wallet upside down and shakes it. Out flies a small, smooth stone, brown with black rings, a tiger's eye. My worry stone that must have been jammed into a far corner. I assumed it was lost and gone. Finally satisfied, the guard hands me my empty bag. I have to scoop all my belongings up and dump them loose into my bag.

Inside, I am directed down a long corridor I haven't yet been through, past administrative offices, through a gate and then I'm in a big room with lots of tables and people. I show my pass and sign a log book, putting down Khalil's name. A guard points to an empty table.

Visitors and prisoners may not touch. You may not give the prisoner anything except by way of a guard.

After some time, Khalil weaves his way through clots of couples and women with children to my table. His face is expressionless, except for what may be a tinge of amusement in his eyes. In this huge, open room, echoing with conversations, Khalil looks small, thinner than usual. He nods at me and sits down.

I brought you something that I didn't want to give you in front of everyone. I pull the dictionary out of my bag, bright red, garish against all the grays and browns and blacks.

A guard appears at the table. Like an efficient waiter, he has been watching and knows when he is needed.

I hold my hand up to the guard. Then I take a pen out and write on the inside cover: *To Khalil. May words be your sword and solace. Ariel Tucker.*

I give the dictionary to the guard who ruffles the pages then places it in front of Khalil. He looks down at it. *Just English?* He raises his eyebrows.

I think you're good enough, don't you?

He smiles. *I don't know.*

There's a moment when neither of us says anything. Khalil opens the book and reads the inscription. *Solace?*

Solace is like peace and tranquility. Comfort. Like home, I say, then feel infinitely stupid—Khalil has no home. My hands are twisting the handles of my bag. *I guess I should go.*

Is it hard to emigrate to America? he asks, leaning towards me.

I imagine it is.

Do you know anyone I can write to there?

My answer to this question has to be careful. *Me,* I want to say. *I'm not sure. I'll let you know.* I push my chair back.

Professor Tucker?

Ariel.

Professor Ariel? I have done nothing but be where I shouldn't be.

And I shouldn't be here now, I think.

See you Monday, Khalil. I make my way out. When I glance back, Khalil is still sitting at the table, looking down at the dictionary.

Khalil does not bring his dictionary to class.

Where's your dictionary? I ask him.

It's too heavy to bring to class every day.

A week later I poke my head into M. Hardin's office to ask if there's a tape player, and I see that the education center has acquired a brand new, red dictionary of English. Before the protest has even left my lips, I march over to the shelf and snatch the book up. Sure enough, it's the one I gave to Khalil.

Where did you get this?

It was donated.

I don't think so.

M. Hardin shrugs, but takes the dictionary frorn me and replaces it on the shelf. They aren't allowed to own anything. Even gifts of food are taken by the guards. I bring in cassette tapes of poetry and the BBC news. I don't hide these things, and strangely enough, M. Hardin doesn't question me, but he watches closely when I pack everything up after class.

At the bistro, Hortense says, *Just for your information, we are starting a new policy. Teachers are not to visit prisoners on an individual basis. Just so you know.*

She doesn't look at me when she says this.

When I get back to the apartment that afternoon, Richard is not home. I open all the doors and windows, starting with the kitchen, until I've worked my way around to my bedroom. The cold air slides in. Richard is furious when he gets home, but I laugh as I watch him shut all the windows. He calls me a crazy bitch and orders me to move out.

When I show up for visiting hours the next Saturday, the guard asks me, *What are you here for?*

Je fais une visite.

But you know the rules, he says.

I nod. *I no longer work here.*

He raises his eyebrows but lets me in.

Khalil looks tired, circles under his eyes, his face unshaven. I want to put my hand to his face, feel it prickle my skin.

How are you?

He lifts a shoulder then lets it drop. *I am ready to go. Empty handed. I came with nothing. I leave with nothing. I travel light.*

He tells me that he gets out Monday but the plane leaves Tuesday. An unexplained bureaucratic gap.

Where will you stay?

I don't know. Some people I know in the Goute d'Or. Here even, if I want. He laughs.

Listen, I whisper. *I will give you my passport. You can use it, can't you?* I have heard that American passports are gold on the black market. I search in my bag for paper and pen, then write my address down. A guard hovers nearby. *Here*, I say, and start to push the paper toward Khalil.

No, he says, *I will memorize it.*

I hold the scrap of paper for him to read.

I lean over my balcony railing, sipping Richard's gin. He has found a new hiding place for it behind his Larousse in his room.

The noisy street cleaning vehicles hug the sidewalk, unhurried. The sun disappears behind the neighbors' roofs, its lingering colors smeared between scrawny metal chimneys.

Since Saturday I have imagined over and over again the words we will say to each other, rehearsed them so often in my head that they already feel like memory.

I wake up hours later, my window is shut. Sunlight cuts the air near my head. A shoe steps into the light.

Light is climbing the opposite wall when I finally wake again to hear Richard cursing outside my door. The empty gin bottle lies on the floor.

There is a scuffling sound. Hard-soled shoes on wood. Then knocking.

Before I'm finished dressing, Richard barges into my room. *Where's my gin?*

As if on cue, two gendarmes appear in the doorway and the concierge's small, pinched face peers over their shoulders.

Ariel Tucker?

They ask to see my passport. I'm searching everywhere. They want to know where Khalil is.

I remember our conversation now, surprised by the way it leaps into consciousness like a forgotten dream. I dropped him my key from the balcony, but yet he knocked before coming into my room. He wore a t-shirt and a light jacket, his fingers, as he handed me the keys, shockingly cold. I tried to pour him the last of the gin, but my hands shook and I spilled some on the floor. He drank the gin straight from the bottle. He said, *Why don't you come with me?*

No, that is not what he said.

He said, *Why are you doing this?*

Because, I said, *what else is there to do?*

Before I slipped away, he said, *Where is it?*

I guess he's missed his flight out. He's illegal again. For one night, he was legitimate, a visitor on foreign soil, a tourist even.

I tell the gendarmes that I cannot find my passport. They say I must come with them, and I do.

They open all the doors for me. One after the other.

Pickpocket

At night I hear her bedroom door slide against the carpet. Then a click as the door closes. Her footsteps do not make any sound at all. I close my eyes. I see her tiptoeing down the stairs. I see her slipping out the front door. On the road she runs. She is trying to take off. She is a bird without wings.

She runs until the air cuts her lungs and she has to walk, clothes already sticky with sweat. She gulps air, the smells of moths and damp leaves and cooling tar.

The music is so loud that the air seems to move to its rhythm. But she does not go into the club. In the parking lot, drunken men, their heads still pounding from the disco, slump in their cars. They are waiting, not knowing that they're waiting, but waiting nonetheless. And she finds them, taps lightly on their windows.

I do not know where my sister goes.

Perhaps she runs in the other direction, into the State Park where the trees are darker than the night. Sounds are louder in the park. Dried twigs crack like bones. The wind is a train whistle and the leaves scratch against each other. Something falls with a thump that shakes the ground underneath her feet. Here her heart seems to beat outside of her body. She crawls under the umbrella branches of a bush, where she is invisible, and lets the sounds push their way into her. The cracks and whistles press through her skin. There is nothing to fear when the sounds fill her, when the sounds become her.

Once I asked her where she goes at night. She said, *The same place you go.*

In the morning, Melissa leans against the kitchen counter where coffee percolates into a pot. Her eyes are glassy, unseeing, her t-shirt wrinkled, shorts twisted on her hips. She may still be sleepy, but her mind is focused, I know it must be. She is thinking about the night, how unreal it seems in the morning. She does not look at me. I brush her arm as I get a coffee mug—she flinches and moves away. I disgust her now.

It used to be that I would play the piano, the one in the living room. When I turn the lights on there now, the piano seems to shrink into the corner. All the furniture, the fleur-de-lis sofa, the mahogany secretary, everything looks brand new, dust free. It used to be that I would play the piano and Melissa would sing in a clear, loud voice, a little flat. It used to be that she would sit next to me on the piano bench to play Chopsticks together, and no one would watch, not even our parents. Sometimes I would imagine my father leaning against the doorway, saying, *Listen to that boy play!*

I wait until they are lulled to sleep by the rhythm of the subway and the warmth of light through the window. I wait until they are gazing at the trotting cityscape, eyes fixed on nothing, minds folded into the maze of their interior geographies.

I study people, the way they hold themselves, the way their hair shields their faces or doesn't, how intent they are on newspapers or headphones. I study the way they cross their legs, whether they sniff or cough when they recross their legs, or whether it's a more unconscious gesture, one inspired by the body's pain and stiffness rather than the mind's discomfort.

A man is reading. He never turns a page. His hands, swollen and red from work, are gigantic next to the small paperback book. Long, auburn sideburns disappear under a black leather cap. He must be thinking of his father who lies in a nursing home bed, who can barely speak. His father remembers being a boy, when he caught frogs by an abandoned quarry. He remembers marrying before the war. But these things the father remembers he cannot say. He loses the words in his throat, and other words replace them. He has seen the puzzled look on his son's face—speaking always fails.

What I do is too easy. I ride closely behind the man on the escalator. I act impatient, push by him and take a slender, silver lighter from his packet. Perhaps a gift from his father? Everyone lines up at the turnstiles but me. I hang back at the Add Fare machine. Engraved on the lighter: *Light the way, Alan.*

At night I hear her door brush against the carpet. Then the click of its closing. She goes so light and quick that her feet only graze the top of the rug. She carries her shoes, putting them on once she gets outside. I see her running down the road, winding with it through fields until it meets the state highway. The night air is sweet and cold, burning her lungs. The running has made her leg muscles twitch and her fingers tingle with the sudden rush of blood. She feels dizzy. She feels drunk, the same way she felt that New Year's when we drank champagne in the basement. Above us our mother's animals scrambled and squeaked in their cages. We drank straight from the bottle, laughing at nothing, laughing at everything, the first time she had ever been drunk. She said, *Let's not go to bed. Let's stay up all night.*

I stand in Melissa's room looking for some sign of where she goes at night. One night soon she will go and not come back. I am waiting for that night, not because I want it to come, because I know it will come. Her room looks unlived in. It's too neat. The bed's cover smoothed so well that it looks like stone, blue as slate. A dresser stands in the corner, nothing on it but a small mirror. The desk is cleared of everything but a lamp, the chair pushed in as far as it will go underneath. Where are her things? In the closet there are some skirts, neatly pressed pants, a few blouses, her shoes lined up on the floor. But that is all. This room is where she dresses, nothing else.

My mother chatters away on the couch, talking to her pets. She holds one of the rabbits on her lap and nuzzles its side with her face. . . . *leaves* . . . *alone* . . . *where* . . . I can't hear everything she says. The rabbit fur muffles her voice. The other rabbit thumps against the cage. The guinea pigs squeal for attention. Only Mr. Blue is silent. The rat sits in a cage on top of the mantel. He crouches there and stares sideways. His whiskers move as he works something between his teeth, Mr. Blue reminds me of an old man who chews his own gums, his mouth in constant motion. During the day my sister is motionless. She lies by the pool or stares at the television. I have watched her, waiting for her to move, to scratch or to shift her weight to a more comfortable spot. But I've watched, it seems, for hours and she never even swallows. Perhaps she sleeps. It is safe to sleep by day.

Now my mother is vacuuming with Mr. Blue on her shoulder. She talks, but it's hard to hear over the roar of the vacuum. She is arguing, her face in a frown. Every so often she reaches a hand into her pocket and takes out a piece of cheese for Mr. Blue. In the front hallway I look in her purse. There are old newspaper clippings about Ricky Nelson. She says they dated a long time ago, when she was 20, still a young woman in Belgium, before he came to a fiery end. There is an alligator skin wallet, keys, a tortoise-shell comb, and an unmarked bottle of pills. The same bottle I found last week but now with fewer pills. They are small, round, and white. I put a couple in my pocket, then zip up her purse.

When I'm on the subway, I can hear Melissa whispering in my ear. See that one? she says and nudges me. The one with her knees pressed so tightly together? The one looking at the window? She's really looking at everyone on the subway car. What does she want that she's so scared of it?

A woman stands next to me on the full train. My hand slides quick and close into her bag, a strange bag with lots of colors and sequins. I do not see her, I mean, I don't look directly at her. To do so would ruin everything. I flush, feel the rush of blood to my face and fingers that happens every time. I see her long, black hair and even her face, her high forehead and her dark eyes searching for something to focus on, on faces turned up at advertisements near the ceiling, tilted, as mine is, towards windows that dark subway tunnels turn into mirrors.

I follow the woman with the sequined bag out of the subway. I follow her until she disappears into a store, a basement gallery in a row of townhouses. Around the next corner, I take out her wallet again, made of colorful fabric. A driver's license: Marigold Grey. Did she invent that name? And does her family call her Mari? Or Margie? I hope not Goldie. She lives in northwest, most likely in a brick house, like all the other brick houses there—white columns in front, five bathrooms. Mari is nineteen, too old for me in her own eyes, I don't like it, but I understand. If I brought her home, my mother would be pleased. She would talk even faster, but in a bright-eyed and cheerful way, give Mari a tour of the house, leaving her menagerie for last. Then she would enjoy Mari's horror as Mr. Blue climbed out of his cage.

In Mari's wallet there's a photo, taken in a portrait gallery, of her standing behind her parents. An only child. What would it be like to be an only child, not to have Melissa there nearly all my life? I cannot know. I stroll back by the gate Mari turned into. I go as far as the bus stop halfway down the block. Soon, Mari comes out of the gallery, looking at the ground, returning the way she came, through the gate, past me and to the subway entrance.

She passes close enough for me to reach out and touch her shoulder, but I don't. She does not even glance at me.

Later, I stop at a window display of televisions. The news is on one of the screens. A woman in a black and white suit, short, red hair and no expression, is looking at me. She is talking and behind her is another face, this one of a man, a mug shot, a black man, and he looks pissed. Then the picture changes: a house door, a townhouse door, lacy iron railings on the steps. I am trembling. I am thinking about other people's houses.

— 44 —

Rush hour has thinned out but still there are a lot of people waiting on the platform. The only calm is in a sea of people, on the subway, bodies moving around, changing coming going.

It is dusk when I walk home from the subway stop. Lights are on in the mansions. Even a stone folly has a light in its tower. I stand and look into a three-story brick house. At a table a man sits hunched over something, his back to the window. A woman comes in and speaks to him, asking him, probably, if love is more important than fidelity. But the man doesn't look up. He nods slightly. She looks out the window, straight at me. She marches to the window and closes the curtains in one sharp motion. Stuck in the middle of their lawn is a little metal sign that says: This house protected by Securities, Inc.

The front of our house is dark. Around back I stand by the pool and see my mother fixing dinner. There is light in Melissa's bedroom window. What could she possibly be doing? My mother is making dinner with Mr. Blue on her shoulder, and through the window screens I hear her chattering to him. From the hallway, my father comes into the kitchen. He moves as if he were dragging great blocks of stone. My mother's voice gets louder but they do not look at each other. He pours himself a drink then goes back into the hallway. I sit by the pool. I keep watch.

My father sits on the front stoop, sipping his drink. I have gone inside to watch him. I can see him from my bedroom window if I kneel on a chair and press my forehead to the glass. Above us the stars are dimmed by the lights from the city miles away. The year the comet came, he told me that the light smeared across the sky was made up of gases, that it wasn't solid. I thought he was lying. I thought the constellations a hoax; they took too much imagination. I did not have the appropriate awe. I refused to believe in the heavens. He sees dying lights, stars long ago extinguished, and I see the lights from neighboring houses blink off, blink on, blink off, blink on.

At night I hear the whisper of her door against the carpet. The latch slips into its groove. She moves so quietly that I can hear the sound of air slipping past her body. She is bold tonight. She is rehearsing. There's a car's motor, steady as it idles and then louder when the clutch releases. She turns onto the state highway; she flies down the road, pressing the gas pedal slowly and watching the speedometer needle shake. There are no other headlights on the road. She is not going anywhere, she is leaving us behind. She is flying. In motion, she is happy.

She slows and turns off onto a dirt road skirting a farm. A field of hay. She drives the car over the edge of the field and turns the lights off. The sounds of night come in through the windows: the flutter of feeding bats and the whine of cicadas. She stretches out in the back seat, the leather cool from the wind, squeaking under her weight. She thinks about hands on her body, hands reaching for curves. Her hand goes to her thigh. Between her legs. The bay dust tickles her nose. Bile rises in the back of her throat, then settles.

Where are you going? I say to her in the morning. She ignores me and walks out to the pool. I say, *There are places I refuse to go!*

Today I am trying hard not to go to the subway. I will sit and watch her, not let her out of my sight. But even as I think this, I realize how impossible it is. I lie on a towel by the pool, across the water from her where she stretches out on a lawn chair. I remember once she pinched her finger hard in the metal of the chair. Her pinky bruised a deep purple. When I close my eyes against the sun overhead I see that purple on my eyelids. I hear the sound of rabbit food dropping into a bowl and my mother's murmurs fade in and out. Her voice sounds like words spoken underwater. Melissa and I used to play underwater games. At the bottom of the pool, her hair floated up and around her head like soft seaweed. Bubbles came out of her mouth, a squirting sound and her underwater laughter. When I wasn't looking, she yanked down my swimtrunks. I chased her and untied her bikini top. Her breasts were dark coins then, swelling.

My mother asks, *Where does he go at night?* Does she mean my father or me? My mother is asking Mr. Blue, who sits in her lap working a scrap of food between his front paws and his mouth. I think she is right to ask a rat, to ask an animal that eats and watches all day, smells and listens all night. He knows what is going on.

My mother comes over to me and pats my hip. *I hope you're keeping that in your pocket.* I know she is talking about sex. That's the way she talks about it. Sometimes she says, *People are not rabbits, you know.*

The red tiles of the subway platform are hot under the sun. I close my eyes and see Melissa lying under the same sun, her body limp but her eyelids, though closed, slightly twitching, nervously resting. When I open my eyes there is a man standing near me, staring at the tracks receding to their distant point. He is waiting for that point to expand, miraculously, as the train approaches. The track will look like it is moving toward us, pulling the train to the platform. The man is carrying a backpack. For a second

I have the urge to be carried in his backpack, toted around like a child.

I have gotten a late start. There are hardly any people on the platform and when the train comes everyone gets a seat. I will have to go someplace where there are lots of people during mid-day. Crystal City. The underground shopping mall. It seems easy there, the crush of people, tired, haggard, rushing, window-shopping. But I have to be careful. There are undercovers. They look like shoppers, eating fried chicken at the food court, strolling past the store windows, appearing like everyone else, but watching.

The palm trees are real. I have touched them before. We (other shoppers and I) sit on a circular bench, like so many palm fronds around the tree's trunk A couple sitting next to me speak in another language, a language I don't even know the name of. They speak slowly, then faster. The man lifts and drops a tube of wrapping paper in a shopping bag, an unconscious gesture, lifts and drops. He tells her that memory fades like the scent of perfume. Remembering takes all of his strength. She says that it does not matter, that memory is only a dream and tonight we will dream again. But he is scared of his dreams, and she holds his hand, comforting him without speaking. I lean into the man, reach for the side pocket of his jacket. I ask, *Where did you get that wrapping paper? I like the design.* He turns and looks at me, then pulls the tube farther out of the bag. My hand is mercury. *Yes, yes*, I say. *It's a very nice pattern.* Race cars. Paper for a small boy's present. The man points down the hall. *The stationery store at the end. On the right.* I nod and smile. *Thanks.* I go. Sharp corners of a hard object prick my palm: a small gold box with engraved initials, A Z on the top. Inside, sand.

I spend a long time in the hobby store looking through kaleidoscopes. I look so long that I begin to see faces in the glittery color flakes.

Rush hour, and I am trying not to step on the toes of seated people as the subway rocks and jerks. When the train stops, people swamp the car. The humidity is dizzying. There is nothing to learn from being so tightly close to another human this way. I turn my head away from the strands of someone's hair tickling my face and, over the bumpy landscape of heads, I see my father's profile. He is looking up at the advertisements above the window. Except for his height and his being my father, there is nothing that makes him stand out from the rush hour throng. His light-blue short-sleeved shirt clings to his back with sweat. I start making my way towards him, using the cover of people leaving and boarding at the next stop to get right behind him. As I'm jostled from behind by new riders I press my side into my father's body, feeling the warmth that rises off his moist skin. I take his wallet. The next stop comes quickly. I push through the bodies to get off. The doors close and people squeeze themselves smaller. The train rushes away into the tunnel. I sit on a bench to wait for the next train and go through the identification cards and the family photos, something I used to do as a child while my father rested on the couch, his keys and wallet on the coffee table.

The platform fills up again with people but they walk far around me.

I keep my collection in a box. I don't take it out every day, maybe once a week, at night. I take it out tonight, open it on my bed. There are six wallets, four dark leather, one tan vinyl, and Mari's colorful cloth one. There are two sets of keys, a smooth, flat stone, and the silver lighter. And the gold box, the miniature desert.

She is in the bathroom—I hear the water running, turning off and on. I hear the hum of the ventilating fan. The hum gets louder when she opens the door. I gather my collection back into the shoebox. I call to her. She backs up to the doorway. She is wearing a large white t-shirt that reaches just beyond the tops of her thighs. *What is it?* She is impatient with me. I don't know what it is. I want her to stop at my door, sit on my bed, make fun of me, hit me even. *Where are you going?* I ask. *What do you mean?* she says. *Where are you going tonight?* She yawns and says, *To sleep.*

I wait and wait for the sound of her, but there is nothing. I go to her bedroom and stand outside her door, but there is nothing. The only sounds are the clicks and creaks of a still house at night. I open the door slowly, expecting to catch her dressing. But there is only the simplicity of her room and the shape of her under a sheet. There is nothing on the floor, not even a sock. There is nothing in this room but her.

I kneel beside her bed and rest my head on the mattress. I let only the tips of my fingers touch the sheet at her hip. Nothing else. I stay that way for minutes, hours, the whole night, wishing it were days.

I am too cowardly to leave before she wakes. I hate this in myself, my inability to stop. I am giving her no choice.

When she wakes she reaches for her watch. She sees me and her eyes widen. Then she looks sleepy again, and annoyed. She doesn't even have to tell me to leave.

When I go out, I feel nervous. But I enjoy waiting, watching for someone. A young woman wearing a light, flowery skirt and white blouse, a shiny blue vinyl bag on her shoulder. Blonde head leaning against a metal pole, she seems thoughtful, but she grips the pole hard, securing herself against the train's shaking. The tunnel makes a sharp turn and the train swerves, throwing everyone, including her—she hangs onto the pole but her body swings out. She hardly notices, she still looks dreamy. She bumps into the person behind her. A hand anchors her. When the train stops, she turns around abruptly and gets off. She knows something, something important, I think, something about love. She is going to meet her lover, to tell him this thing she knows. I follow her off the train and up an escalator, running to get right behind her in the line for the turnstile. When she inserts her Farecard, I reach, stretch my fingers into her blue bag, no time to search, just to grab the first object. I am holding a little book, an address book, red with embroidery in a Chinese pattern.

Someone yells out *Hey!* from behind. She turns and sees me holding the book, but I jump the turnstile, run up the stairs and out, run into the crowds of people at Dupont Circle. I turn a corner, pass a McDonald's and enter a bookstore, pocketing the address book. I stand behind a bookcase. I am facing the windows, pretending to inspect the back cover of a novel. Outside, the girl and a security cop come running around the corner. They stop, search for me. I'm surprised they don't think of looking in this shop. Instead they talk. He writes something in a little notebook. She stays in place for a moment, peering at passing male faces. She gives up, crosses the street, and I watch her head bob away into the crowd of other bobbing heads.

The names and addresses are written in a neat, angular print, in pencil. Everything in capital letters. There are at least a hundred names in this book, but not hers. Of course not hers.

At night I hear the whisper of the door against the thick carpet of her bedroom. There is no other sound. She tiptoes down the stairs, her shoes in one hand, a sweater in the other. The nights are cooler now. She does not run. Tonight she will walk and never stop walking. She will walk until she becomes a tiny point in the distance, disappearing like faces in a kaleidoscope, except for the memory of her I keep squeezed in my fists, my fists deep in my pockets.

The Bad Luck Gods

I t was August when Cheryl first saw the parakeet. Indigo buntings, goldfinches, cardinals with their crimson feathers, iridescent grackles—they all strutted their exotic fashions at the bird feeder every day. But the parakeet's yellow and blue stood out like the Sugar Plum Fairy among the snowflakes.

He sat on a low branch over the deck, head twitching, waiting his turn but keeping at least one eye on every movement. Cheryl shouted for her daughter to come see.

"Hold on," Viv murmured, her zombie-eyes fixed on the computer screen where she was playing Minecraft.

How Cheryl hated the game that stole her daughter's mind. "No!" she said. "Come here, now!"

Something in her tone must have frightened her daughter for Viv was by her side in a shot. Perhaps she thought it was another bear, like the one they had seen galloping from the side of the house the previous fall. Or a moose like the one they almost crashed into one icy day in February.

"What? What?" Viv said breathlessly.

"Look." Cheryl pointed, but just as she did, the parakeet flew off.

"Oh," Viv said, disappointed. "It's just a bird."

"It's a parakeet!"

"So?"

"It's not supposed to be flying free." The truth was only just hitting Cheryl as she said it. That was someone's pet.

"It's not?" Viv pushed her nose against the screen, as though somehow she would be able to understand her mother's concern better by doing that.

"It must have escaped," Cheryl explained.

Viv shrugged, then returned to virtual reality.

In the shed, Cheryl dug through a bin of plastic buckets, broken sand shovels, deflated beach balls, badminton rackets, and grimy bubble wands, the backyard equivalents of unpaired socks. She was looking for the butterfly nets Viv had long ago used to catch frogs. Viv would stand on the little wood pier that jutted into their swampy pond, craning over the duck weed-speckled water for hours, in June when the tadpoles were still only wiggly commas, in July as the tadpoles sprouted stumpy legs and their tails shrank. Whenever Cheryl looked up from the kitchen window or the screened porch, there Viv was, kneeling by the pond or bent over a bucket. If Ricky was outside mowing, Viv showed him every find, and he always paused the mower to peer into a bucket, even though it meant several minutes of coaxing the cranky engine back to life.

The memory of Ricky stopped Cheryl short. A sand bag of grief walloped her chest. She gripped the edge of a recycling container to steady herself.

The nets were propped in a dark corner of the shed behind a tangle of garden rakes and shovels. One of the nets was torn, so she left it there, scolding herself for not putting it in the garbage, and then scolding herself again for not thinking of something creative and fun to recycle it into. That kind of thing had always been Ricky's job.

She waited on the porch with the good net in hand. The parakeet chirped faintly in one of the trees at the edge of the pond. She imagined he needed the feeder. Where else would he find food? Would he even have a clue how to eat in the wild? She wondered all sorts of things: Can parakeets smell? How far can they see? Could they understand what other birds were saying? Was this parakeet bewildered, or was he drunk on his new freedom? Was he a *he*? If someone lost a parakeet, how would they advertise it? People put homemade signs up on the trees in the neighborhood when their cats and dogs went missing. Sometimes the signs stayed up for months, faded and streaked by rain, forgotten by owners who had abandoned their searches. But she had never seen a sign for a bird.

From the tall maple tree by the pond, an arrow of yellow shot out and swooped toward the deck. He landed on a nearby branch. She held her breath. He flew to the feeder. She reached a hand to the screen door, but the hinge squeaked when she pushed it open and the parakeet zoomed off.

"You've been on that computer for nearly three hours. It's time to be done."

"I'm almost done."

"That's what you said over an hour ago."

"But I am. Almost done."

"If you don't shut it down now, I'm going to do it myself." She stepped toward the metal computer desk where her daughter sat hunched over the laptop.

"Mom! Don't! I'm saying goodbye now."

"You were saying goodbye an hour ago. This is the millionth

time I've asked you to turn it off. Why does it take you so long to say goodbye?"

A shrug. Then Viv closed the laptop with a soft click. Cheryl resolved—also for the millionth time—to register for Minecraft and play herself, something one of the therapists had suggested. *If you see it from her perspective and share in the experience, then it doesn't have to become such a point of tension*, Dr. Wiggan had said. While they were in therapy, she fantasized about recording the arguments she had with Viv to play back in the session. Why did the advice seem so reasonable in the therapist's office, with the calming sound of the noise machine just outside the door, while in the middle of an argument, her head bursting with anger, the calm of the therapist's office felt as far away as India?

Last winter, before the accident, she had planned her leaving over and over again. Sometimes it was merely a fantasy. In the car, speeding away from the house, her heart racing, she imagined checking into the Holiday Express, sprawling across the crisp, bleached sheets of a hotel room bed, and soaking up solitude. But, in calmer moments, when she realized that the years of tension and arguments had suffocated her feelings for Ricky, she imagined a more likely reality: tears, boxes, moving vans, and lawyers.

It wasn't his fault. It wasn't her fault. They had poured all the energy of their 30s and early 40s into parenting. They were exhausted, sapped. The image of dried cornstalks in late November came to mind.

She faced the fact that she was out of her league with the parakeet. She would have to call in the Bird Lady of Barnsville. *The Barnsville Record* had once run a front page feature about the Bird Lady, who kept rescue parrots and a white cockatoo that bleated "I love you." The Bird Lady also ran a pet care business so Cheryl looked her up in the old-fashioned phone book that she still used—which Viv rolled her eyes at—but otherwise was rapidly becoming extinct, like typewriters and public phones. The Bird Lady said she'd stop by on her way back from her afternoon client visits. By "client," the Bird Lady meant furry creatures whose human companions were vacationing at the Cape or on African safaris or somewhere else exotic and far away from home.

While she waited for the Bird Lady, Cheryl logged onto Craigslist to post a notice about the parakeet. First, she looked through the previous week's listings to see if anyone was looking for a lost parakeet. There were a few missing Chihuahuas, which seemed to get lost more easily than other dogs. A couple of lost cats. Someone trying to sell a spider and lots of posts looking to "rehome" pets. Hers would be the only notice that week for a parakeet, or a bird of any kind.

Viv was still glued to her computer screen. Cheryl watched her trying to make her avatar jump up onto high ledges while upbeat music pulsed from the computer. Viv held her left arm out to the side, waving it like she was trying to fly. Cheryl wondered if such unconscious flapping counted as exercise.

She was about to tell her daughter to turn the game off, when a silver VW bug pulled up in the driveway. "Punch buggy. One, two, three!" she yelled and gave Viv a light punch to the shoulder.

"What?" Viv said, her eyes not leaving the screen.

"There's a VW bug in our driveway."

She glanced out the window. "Oh," she said, returning to her video game.

Cheryl leaned down to whisper in her ear. "I'm going to text all of your friends from your phone to tell them how much you love me."

"Okay, Mom," Viv said, her tone of voice indicating she would roll her eyes if they weren't so busy with her video game.

The Bird Lady's name was Martha, the kind of name you'd never hear in birth announcements these days. A beautiful, solid name, not like Brittany or Sophia or Ashley. Cheryl thought there should be seasonal quotas on baby's names, like with hunting. Only so many could be culled from the list of names per year. And certain overly precious names, such as Lyric and Summer, should be considered too endangered to use at all. Heavy fines, maybe even federal prison time, if you named your baby after flowers or fruit.

Martha was a large woman with a sweet smile and friendly eyes to match. She wore her long dark hair down even in the heat of the day.

"Thanks for stopping by," Cheryl said, inviting Martha in. She led the Bird Lady through the living room, flicking a hand in the direction of her daughter. "That's Viv. She donated her brain to the video game industry." Martha chuckled, which Cheryl appreciated.

Out on the deck, she showed Martha the feeder and the tree where she had first seen the parakeet. She sheepishly pointed to the net, anticipating that Martha would scoff.

Martha nodded, which Cheryl took as reassurance that she wasn't completely off base with the net. "Are you able to get close to it?" Martha asked.

"Not really. When I tried, it flew up into that tree." She pointed to a tall maple at the edge of the lawn.

"If it can fly that high," Martha said, "it's been out and about for a while and its wings have become stronger. A caged bird's wings are clipped so it can't fly that high."

"Oh. Do you think there's any way to catch him?"

Martha bit her lip, thinking. "I'll tell you what," she said. "If you get a large net, the kind that you might put on berry bushes to keep birds out, you could try to throw it over the bird when it's at the feeder."

Ricky had planted blueberry and raspberry bushes a few years back and had always talked about getting nets to keep the birds out, but he never did. Every summer the bushes grew a little bigger, the branches burst with more berries, and just as the hard green fruit ripened the birds stripped the bushes clean.

After dinner, she and Viv went to the discount store Big Lots. They cruised the aisles of inner tubes and cat litter, spiral notebooks and picnic gear. There was no logic to the arrangement of things, which was part of the fun. You never knew what you might find next to the $3 t-shirts, Easter baskets, soap holders, rakes. Finally, squeezed between the flip flops and boxes of wine glasses, they spied garden nets. Viv also found glow-in-the-dark silly putty.

On the way home, they passed the Bay Street Cemetery. Everyone said it would get easier with time, but it hadn't yet. Viv was silent in the back of the car. Used to be that she'd hold her breath and lift her feet until they had passed by a cemetery. "It's bad luck if you don't," she'd say. But Viv didn't do that anymore. She had given up on placating the bad luck gods.

The shock of Ricky's dying was too much to bear at first, and Cheryl knew she was not as attentive to Viv as her daughter probably needed her to be. Friends of Ricky's from work brought food and attended the wake and funeral. His parents had already passed. Her parents flew out from Arizona for a couple weeks and took Viv under their wing, but they eventually had to leave. Ricky's friends went on with their lives. Both Ricky and she were in their late twenties when they met, and after Viv was born Cheryl had taken leave from her crappy administrative assistant job and decided not to go back. Work friendships eventually faded without the daily interactions that anchored those relationships. Then, one day several weeks after the funeral, Cheryl got up from her morning nap which had turned into an afternoon nap and realized that Viv and she were alone together.

When they got home from Big Lots, Viv ran upstairs to her

room to see if the putty actually glowed in the dark. In the waning sunlight, Cheryl opened the box that held the net. It was a big net. She could fit it over her head and it still draped down to the floor like an oversized wedding veil. It would need to be tacked or nailed to a frame of some sort.

The parakeet chirped somewhere in the trees at the edge of the yard, a voice in the wilderness of crickets and cicadas.

That night, she lay in bed, thinking about the woodshop above the garage. Ricky would disappear up there for hours, then emerge with a bookshelf or a picture frame. She hadn't been in the shop since before the accident. There had to be wood she could use for framing. She had vague memories of scraps of two-by-fours and sawdust littering the floor. But she couldn't remember what else was there besides the saws and planers. She imagined holding a hammer in her hand, the cold weight of its steel head, the satisfaction of a clean strike on a nail. Metal and wood: She envied the simplicity of their relationship.

She woke early the next morning. Viv had taken to sleeping in and Cheryl dreaded what it would take to wake her for the first days of school.

The coffee dripped into its pot. She liked the smell of it better than the taste. Still, she drank it. Ricky would go through two pots a day. When he tried to cut back he'd get withdrawal headaches. She and his brother had joked at the funeral that they should have buried a coffee maker with Ricky, or maybe a mug, because, surely, there would be limitless free coffee in heaven.

With a cup in hand, she climbed the stairs to the workshop over the garage and pressed the door latch. The workshop felt empty and silent, even more so than in the house those first few days after the funeral. In the house, everyday sounds broke the silence—the bleeps of the computer, the toilet flushing, feet slapping up and down the stairs. But here in the workshop, where Ricky had been the primary occupant, the emptiness hit her in the gut. The sobs rose up in her throat without warning. As though someone had kicked her from behind, she fell to her knees and the coffee spilled across the floor, a dark stain that soaked into the wood shavings.

She squeezed her eyes shut. She had turned down the friendly offers—"Let me know what I can do"—phrases that rang over and over again in her head. Pamphlets on grieving and support groups piled up in the recycling. She knew people meant well, that she would do the same if the roles were reversed. Still, a huge gulf had opened up between her and them, too wide to cross with hope of ever returning.

She opened her eyes and took a deep breath, inhaling the clean wood smell edged with coffee. For a moment she couldn't remember what she was doing there. She sat back on her heels and noticed the red plastic-covered couch they had brought home years ago from the swap station at the landfill. In Ricky's mind, there was almost nothing that couldn't be fixed or reused. How much money he had saved them over the years, she couldn't begin to calculate.

Once she stood up, she felt better, her head cleared. She gathered up the wet sawdust into the mug. The table saw was in the middle of the room, still covered in wood dust; discarded wood pieces with splintered edges lay like casualties on its surface. She skated her hand across the cold, smooth surface of the saw table's blade guard, clearing a path through the dust. Then, with her index finger, she touched the point of one tooth in the blade. Still as sharp as a razor. Her finger turned white where the tooth dimpled the flesh, and then the skin blossomed red as blood rushed to the almost-wound.

More painful than losing him somehow was picturing him taking his final breath alone in his crumpled Ford pickup truck, the whine of a faraway ambulance the last sounds he heard. It was only recently she had stopped constantly imagining his last moment. A whole day could go by without the image swooping into her mind. Now, she pressed the imaginary remote control that turned it off. That's what one of the pamphlets had suggested and surprisingly it worked.

In the far corner there stood about a dozen or so lengths of wood of varying heights. She picked out the four tallest ones and left.

In the house Viv swayed in her nightgown in the kitchen, still waking up. "Where were you?" she whined.

"Getting these." She indicated the wood.

"What for?"

"The net." She leaned the wood up against a wall. Viv scrunched her face in confusion. "To frame the net." Viv tilted her head. "You know, you have to have something to shape the net, like the one you used to catch frogs."

"Whatever." Viv shrugged and headed towards the refrigerator.

With a hammer and a staple gun Cheryl assembled the frame on the deck. The small shocks of impact—hammer to nail, staple into wood—reverberated through her arms. The birds were squawking and chirping in the canopy of nearby maple trees, keeping a cautious distance from the feeder while she worked. She punched the last staple into the frame and picked up the net. It was very awkward and would require two hands to maneuver.

Later that day the Bird Lady stopped by. Cheryl showed her the net. "You've been busy," Martha said cheerfully.

They walked the yard looking for the parakeet. Viv had decided that for once what her mother was doing was more interesting than the computer, so she watched the search from the deck. Martha stopped under a five-story tall swamp maple that dripped its thickly leafed branches over the pond and aimed her binoculars into its canopy.

"There it is," she said, pointing and handing Cheryl the binoculars.

Up close, the parakeet's blue and yellow feathers looked especially bright against the leaves. His head twitched and tilted, trying to see everything. Why had he escaped? Did animals have the urge, like humans did, to go beyond their capabilities? Had the parakeet flown out of the cage to see a nearby tree, and then flown farther to see what was at the next tree, and the next, and the next? When hunger struck, had the parakeet looked back and realized he had lost his way? Did he sense, like wild birds, the seasons changing, the certainty of fall, then winter's arrival?

Cheryl knew it wasn't going to be easy but she hadn't realized how hard it would be. The optimal time to try to catch the bird was probably the early morning, just at sunrise, when he was hungry from a night of fasting. After a couple of mornings of complete failure, she figured she should be out *before* sunrise, while it was still dark, so the parakeet couldn't see her emerging from the door and crouching on the deck. Cheryl squatted next to the feeder, trying to find a position that wouldn't tire her too soon but would also enable her to move quickly when she needed to. Holding a four-foot net didn't make it any easier. She would just have to hope that parakeets couldn't smell or see too well. Trying to ignore how foolish she felt and the burning sensation in her knees, she waited.

The dark of night faded into the gray of early morning. After what seemed to be an hour, but was probably only five minutes, the familiar chirping noise of the parakeet drew near. It landed on a far branch of a young redbud tree, scoping out the situation. The more motionless Cheryl tried to be, the more her hands shook. Her nose itched. The bird flew towards the feeder just as Cheryl sneezed. It was gone in an instant. She cursed the bad luck gods and stomped into the house.

It was Viv's first day of tenth grade and she was deep in slumber. Cheryl stood at the end of the bed for a moment, watching her daughter's slack face and the gentle rhythm of her breathing, the rise and fall of her blue top sheet.

Her girl was still amazing to her. Cheryl hoped she always would be. It sometimes hit her in the gut that Viv was hers, that she had given birth to this person who was a wholly separate human being from her. The last thought frightened her. Every day, it seemed, Viv became more separated from her. As a baby, she had always wanted to be held. She nursed until she was two. She hated to be in strollers, always wanted to be carried. Eventually she was too big for carrying, but she still wanted to crawl into Cheryl's lap at inconvenient times, dinner, at the movies. Soon she was too big for that. At nine and ten, Viv still grasped her mother's hand to cross the street and they gave each other a kiss in the morning and at night. But now—it had been weeks since the last time Viv had offered her a cheek to be kissed or opened her arms to invite a hug. Cheryl held on to the memory of her baby curled on her chest, Viv's sweat breath warm on her neck, though it was dissipating with every day.

For the first days after Ricky's accident, she was afraid to let Viv out of her sight. Viv had clung to her, too, and she ricocheted between grief and delight in her daughter's closeness, but eventually Viv relaxed into a more casual distance. Cheryl realized how much her husband had been a cushion between her and Viv, for better or worse. Ricky had called her controlling, which stung, because she realized it was partly true. With Ricky there, she had let him do the heavy lifting, so to speak, to avoid the constant tension and bickering between her and her daughter. But it also meant a cushion against the good stuff, what often came unexpectedly, like the way Viv let Cheryl hold her in those days after the funeral.

Viv's eyes fluttered and opened. She lifted her head to look at Cheryl and then slumped back into her pillow.

"Mom," she said. "What are you doing?"

Cheryl playfully pinched Viv's toes. "I'm watching over Sleeping Beauty," Cheryl said as cheerily as she could muster but it caught in her throat, still thick with emotion.

"Mom," she moaned, meaning, "Don't be corny, Mom."

In the kitchen, she got out bowls, cereal, and orange juice. Viv dragged herself in and stood rubbing her eyes.

"It's your first day of tenth grade," Cheryl said. "Aren't you excited?"

Viv yawned. "Not really. Same old same old."

"You're too young to be jaded," she said, pouring juice.

Later, Viv stood in the driveway, her new backpack draped over one shoulder and scrawled with peace signs in fabric marker. Cheryl thought of the last time Viv had waited for the bus, in June, on the final day of school. She wondered if her daughter was thinking of the same thing: they had waited in innocence that morning, not knowing at the end of the day Ricky would be gone.

The bus exhaled to a stop, like a yellow dragon, at the end of the driveway. Viv waved her hand over her shoulder at her mother. From an outsider's perspective the wave might have seemed lackluster, but to Cheryl it was infused with everything.

That day she checked her e-mail too many times, hoping for some response to the Craigslist ad. Worried that she had made a mistake while posting it, she went back into the post and double-checked that she had followed the instructions correctly. She had. The post was there. It was just that no one was looking for a lost parakeet. Either that or someone was looking but hadn't yet checked Craigslist. Maybe the bird had flown from farther away than the surrounding community. Maybe this bird had traveled across state lines.

She half-heartedly checked the help wanted ads online. She knew that wasn't really how you got a job but at least it made her feel like she was doing something. After lunch she took her coffee on the deck, careful not to let the door creak too loudly. Maybe if the parakeet got used to her presence, it would visit the feeder even if she was visibly nearby.

She settled into one of the green plastic fake Adirondack chairs, which weren't all that comfortable with their sharp edges. Nonetheless, in the late summer sun she soon dozed. When she woke a few minutes later, her neck kinked from its odd angle, the parakeet was there, at the feeder. She stilled herself, planning her moves. The net was by the side of her chair, but she'd have to lean over to pick it up and would most likely startle the bird.

In that moment, as she sat paralyzed with indecision, the certainty of her failure strangely relaxed her. Her muscles, taut with her previous eagerness to act, softened and she relaxed against the deck chair.

The parakeet pecked nervously at the feeder, hopping from perch to perch, jerking and angling its yellow-feathered head in a constant effort to keep her in sight.

When Viv came home that afternoon, she mumbled a greeting on her way toward the computer.

"How was your first day?"

"Good."

"What did you do?"

"Stuff."

Cheryl sighed. Viv sat down at the computer and logged on, her attention completely absorbed by the screen.

"No homework?" Cheryl waited for a response but got none. "Vivian!"

Viv looked up in surprise, then registered Cheryl's question and shook her head.

Two weeks later with still no sign of homework, Cheryl checked Viv's grades online and discovered that there was a long line of zeros in her daughter's assignments record.

She considered her options. She could stop paying the cable bill. As it was, the life insurance would last only a few more months with current expenses. But since it was the beginning of the month, the cable was paid up for the next four weeks.

She could change the wifi password. She'd never done that. Ricky had taken care of getting the wifi installed and setting up passwords. But there had to be a manual somewhere. Or, better yet, she could Google it, which she did and found the instructions. The new password was parakeet52.

That afternoon when Cheryl heard the bus sigh to a stop and then whine back into gear, she steeled herself for Viv's reaction. "Hey, Mom," Viv said, entering the house. She threw her backpack on the couch and stopped at the refrigerator for a glass of orange juice.

"Hi, Sweetie." Cheryl wiped down the already clean counter while Viv settled herself at the computer.

"What's this?" Viv said and twisted around in the chair to look at her mother.

"There's a new password."

"Why?" Viv waved her hands at Cheryl with impatience.

"Because I checked your grades on Power School and it looks like you've not been doing your homework."

"I *have*!"

"Then why are there so many zeros?"

Viv scowled at Cheryl. "My teachers don't like me."

"How do you know?" Cheryl rinsed the sponge and set it on the soap dish. She was trying to stay cool. Calm and collected.

She crossed her arms and leaned up against the wall, hoping that her position communicated detached authority.

Viv shrugged.

"Perhaps if you did your homework they would like you."

"What's the point?"

"Of what?"

"Of homework!"

"Why are you doing this, Viv?"

"I'm not doing anything."

"Why are you not doing your school work?"

"It doesn't matter," Viv said and slumped in the chair.

"School?"

"All of it!"

Cheryl hesitated, then dove in. "Is this about your father?"

Viv didn't respond.

"Listen," she said, approaching her daughter. She knelt down by Viv's chair and put a hand on her daughter's slender arm, still brown from summer. Viv shifted out from under her hand. "Your dad wouldn't want you to give up, would he?"

Viv's shoulders shook and she bowed her head, a waterfall of hair shielding her face. Then Viv jumped up from the chair and ran upstairs to her room. Cheryl felt the slam of the door vibrate through her knees.

Martha called that night to check in and Cheryl gave her an update, which was not really an update, but a continuation of the same. The next day the Bird Lady stopped by and they walked around the yard but there was no sign of the parakeet. Eventually Martha's calls and visits stopped.

October brought cooler mornings. Cheryl still took her coffee out to the deck after the bus picked up Viv. Occasionally she saw a blue and yellow streak swoop across the trees.

One morning in early November the newspaper warned the

first serious frost might happen that night. Cheryl spent the day checking on the feeder, walking the perimeter of the yard a few times, in between writing cover letters and tweaking her very thin resume. The parakeet was nowhere to be seen.

She tried to look free from worry that afternoon as Viv hopped down the school bus steps and into the driveway. Viv was waving a green piece of paper.

"There's going to be a play!" she shouted. She shoved the paper at Cheryl along with her backpack. "I want to try out."

"Of course," Cheryl agreed cautiously, afraid too much enthusiasm on her part might backfire.

In the house, Viv chirped away about the play and her friends who were going to audition too. For once, she didn't run directly to the computer. She chattered about which outfit she would wear to the audition and which song she would sing. For a few minutes that afternoon Cheryl felt something like joy again, infected by her daughter's excitement.

After Viv was tucked into bed, Cheryl perched on a deck chair, arms clutching her torso, and shivered in her thin sweater. It wouldn't appease the bad luck gods, but she closed her eyes anyway and lifted her feet off the deck.

The parakeet flew in gentle swoops, arcing away from her toward the tallest tree in the yard and far beyond, going farther than he ever had before.

Don't Go

Darren looked up at the sky, a field of white in the glare of the sun. From this angle, stretched out across the roof, he could almost pretend the flood hadn't happened.

The smoke from Phoebe's cigarette curled down to him. She hugged her knees, the way she used to hug him on the Harley, and stared at the watery field across the road. The swollen river had deposited the work van in the field, its front pointed away from them, as though it had been abandoned by a driver who'd had one too many.

"God's trying to tell me something," she said. "You belong in the desert. That's what He's saying."

His golden girl from Nevada. A family of sheepherders. Phoebe knew the desert better than most, which plants were edible, which were poisonous, which held water during the driest stretches. She could handle living with next to no water.

He closed his eyes against the glare and felt her arms around him again, her cheek against his shoulder, and the way the wind whipped his face when they rode.

They had met in a bar near her reservation five years ago, while he was on a Harley trip in the southwest. Sweet nights he couldn't shake from memory back in Tennessee. When the repair jobs died down in late fall, he got back on his bike. This time he convinced her to move to Tennessee.

Almost overnight in the humidity her straight hair curled up into bouncy ringlets and curvy wisps around her face.

It had rained sheets. Flood warnings came over the radio every ten minutes or so, in between the "oldies but goodies." On the front porch, water cascaded from the gutters and clung to the screens, a blinding cataract. It was impossible to see how far the river had come up the gravel embankment.

He worried about the basement. The circuit breaker was about five feet from the basement floor. The river had flooded before but had never gotten that high. But it also had never rained this long and hard either.

Earlier that morning, figuring they had a few hours before the river rose over the lip of their sloped lawn, he and Phoebe had emptied the basement freezer, moved it to the front porch, and then repacked it. They had lugged boxes—mostly his things, honorable discharge papers, and various electrical training manuals—up to the attic crawl space. He slid the old photo album into a freezer bag and put it on the counter next to another bag with his phone and cigarettes.

They had restacked the wood pile on higher ground near the road. They had re-parked the pickup and Phoebe's car onto the road above the house. The Harley wasn't around to worry about, sold off in a lean year. The work van didn't run so it sat between the river and house, its hood open, tools scattered around it, like some sort of prehistoric bird waiting to be fed. He had gathered up the tools and stored them in the pickup underneath their kayaks. The river was the reason he bought the property. Nothing particularly special about the house, a one-story ranch with an unfinished basement. But in the back there was a wide yard and the river beyond that, its current fast and strong during the spring thaw, gentler but still cooling in summer. An old maple— trunk too wide for him to reach around—draped its branches over the embankment, providing blessed shade in July. Under the maple's canopy, he and Phoebe had said their vows. Nearby, on a metal rack, they stored their canoe and kayaks. It was easy to slide them into the river. All you needed was a cooler of beer and sandwiches.

They did everything on the river. Cookouts. Fishing. Kayaking. He could come home for lunch while rewiring someone's attic and in three seconds be in the water, floating on his back, the sky overhead, hearing the smack of the screen door as Phoebe came out to greet him.

At night there was nothing more soothing than sitting by the water, a beer in one hand, a cigarette in the other, and Phoebe searching the rocky bank for round stones. The fireflies blinked in the dark, stars fallen to earth.

But beauty and tranquility always came with a price.

Mercy, their retriever, now barked at the screen door. "What is it, girl?" Phoebe asked, kneeling down to sink her fingers into the dog's black fur.

Darren stepped out to the deck, ducking fast by the sheet of water pouring off the gutter. The rain slapped his head and face.

The river had slid over the embankment into the yard, surrounding the base of the maple. Their geese huddled under the deck and he could sense them there, honking and flapping their worry.

When he came back inside, Phoebe greeted him with a dry towel. He didn't bother changing clothes this time. He was soaked and he would stay soaked.

She looked at him expectantly, sucking on her cigarette.

"It's up to the tree," he said, toweling his hair.

Phoebe stubbed her cigarette out in the ashtray on the kitchen counter. She went to the bedroom and came out a few seconds later carrying her suitcase and the bird cage. Baby the cockatiel squawked and fluttered.

He couldn't help but think this is how she would look when she left him.

He fussed with the stove, making sure everything was disconnected. Mercy stood at attention at his feet.

He took the suitcase and opened the front door, hesitating a moment before ducking into the pounding rain, with Mercy and Phoebe following. He didn't need to look to know that all the seedlings Phoebe had planted in the yard had long washed away.

Inside the truck the windows fogged up instantly. He turned the ignition and soon the heat was blowing, enough to keep Phoebe and Mercy from shivering. "What about Amber and Cat?" Phoebe said.

"They're cats. They'll climb trees."

She frowned.

"How can we find them now?" he pleaded. They were part feral, those cats. There was no way to get them in the truck.

He turned the windshield wipers on as fast as they would go, which allowed him a blinking view of the truck hood. Hoping to get to his father's house in Granville, about ten miles away, they crawled toward the main road but as soon as they got there they could see the way was washed out in the direction of Granville. He turned left, instead of right, and they drove toward the Walmart on the county line.

He had to hand it to her. Moving a thousand miles from where you've lived your whole life to be with a near stranger? Not an easy thing. It had taken some work on his part. Phone calls. Letters. Photos. Lots of photos. Of the house and river, geese, yard, the rolling hills that took you up to great heights over the kudzu-choked landscape and down into the shaded hollers.

Would he have traded all that—plus his father and brother—for the desert? Long stretches of dry flatness made to seem all the more flat by the occasional mesas that punched up out of the land. The scent of sage in the cool mornings. The relief of sunset, a smear of color across the horizon.

It was lovely to visit, but live there? Plus, he had built up his business from scratch over the years. He was too old to pull up stakes and try to find a new customer base.

All this he explained to her on the phone. There had been one conversation, after the first trip to New Mexico, when he thought she was close to deciding. He'd had a couple beers and when he called a man answered the phone. It could've been one of her brothers or nephews.

"Darren," she said, when she got on the phone. "Why did I know it was you?"

"Maybe," he said, "because even on the phone I'm sooooo gooood lookin'!"

She laughed, the sound of which was almost as delicious to him as her lips on his.

"Who answered the phone?"

"Why? Are you the jealous type?"

"Just wondered if it was someone I met."

"Don't know," she said. "Did you meet Angelo?"

He hadn't met that brother, or, if he had, he couldn't remember. She teased him about his poor memory. There was only a ten-year difference in their ages and, like him, she had been married once before. A childhood friend, but they had decided they were better suited as friends than lovers, she'd told him.

Phoebe said she had been researching plants native to western Tennessee. She gathered medicinal plants, as her mother had taught her and her mother's mother had taught her. He had been impressed by her ability to look across the desert landscape and know what grew where.

"Ginseng," she said. "That grows out by you."

After they had hung up he went and stood by the river, a cigarette in one hand, a beer in the other. It was late and he could hear the river more than he could see it, a low whooshing sound as it came around the bend, running white and shallow over the rocks, and then gurgling into a deep pool on the other side where he had hung a rope swing.

He put out his cigarette and left the empty beer can on the bank. The water was the same temperature as the steamy July night air. When the nights got cooler and deer season opened he would go up to the hunting camp.

In one spot the water came up to his neck. He ducked his head under and floated there for a second, letting the current carry him down river a few feet. He dragged his foot along the river bank until he felt a jutting rock, then grabbed a thick root above it and hauled himself up out of the water. On this side, the clay was orange and the bank steep. He reached for the roots that made a natural ladder and pulled himself up to the ledge. Behind the plant growth was a small trail packed down by feet on countless summer days of hanging out at the river. He still couldn't see well and had to rely on his instinct to know how far he was from the ledge and the tree with the rope.

In the faint glow of his house lights, he could just make out the dark outline of the rope tree, one sturdy trunk arched over the river.

But he miscalculated the edge of the bank and when he reached for the rope his foot stepped into air. He slid down, scraping his hands against rocks and roots, and tumbled into the water. The splash disturbed something in the bushes. Sputtering water and shaking his head, he heard the creature rustling off into the trees.

If Phoebe had been there, she'd have just laughed herself silly. Imagining her laughing at him had made him hoot out loud, and he heard a return hoot from his neighbor Jimmy who was probably sitting in the dark on his porch a hundred feet or so up the river.

"Sound like you all caught a biggun'!" Jimmy hollered, then cackled.

"Except it got away, man!" he yelled back.

Even when he thought he was alone, he wasn't. But the thought hadn't cheered him. Jimmy was a real drunkard and took to shooting animals that wandered onto his property.

Darren slowly pushed across the current and reached the river bank. The breeze had shifted and the mosquitoes were torrential so he hot-footed across the gravel and the lawn and into the house, where Mercy sat just inside the door, waiting for him.

When Jimmy had shot at Cat, Phoebe had wanted to call the police on him, but Darren said it would only make things worse. She knew he was right. When Jimmy drank, he had a mean streak. Never knew what could happen. What with the neighbor, the lost babies, Darren gone all day long at work, and now the flood—it was a small miracle Phoebe had stayed as long as she did.

He'd never seen rain like this. It was slow going on the road. The visibility was next to zero. As they got farther down the county road, there were more cars. Mercy panted in the backseat and Phoebe twisted in her seat to look at the dog. "She can't be hot. Must just be worry."

The Walmart lot was nearly full but they squeezed into a space in a far corner between the edge of the asphalt and an old

'70s-era station wagon with wood paneling. He wasn't too sure it was the best place to be in a flood but it was still on the highest land in the county. On the radio, there was talk of releasing the dam. He shut off the radio.

His cell phone chirped.

"Hey, Dad, are you staying dry?"

"Not too bad." Thankfully, his father lived on top of a hill near TVA land and no rivers. "How's your place?"

"Not good," he said. "We're in the Walmart parking lot!" He had to yell into the phone to be heard over the pounding rain.

"Mercy's here with us. Don't know where the cats got to."

"Did you get the photos out?" his father asked.

Oh fuck! He'd forgotten the photos.

There was a silence on the line and then his dad said, "That's all right," though they both knew it wasn't.

His father changed the subject. "Did you hear about the dam?"

"If they open it, we're goners."

"They gotta save Nashville," his father said sarcastically.

"That's right. Us ridge runners ain't worth nothing!"

"I talked to Tommy."

"How's he holding up?"

"He's fine," his father said, sounding annoyed that his youngest son was not in danger, not forced to prove his manhood. "He's at work and you know they don't build any state offices in the flood plains."

"Shoot! That's for sure."

After the conversation with his father, Darren watched cars circling at a snail's pace around the parking lot. He couldn't believe he'd forgotten the photos. He'd grabbed the bag with his phone and cigarettes, but not the one with the album.

Phoebe had been quiet, smoking the entire time he was talking to his father. Now, she put her hand on his arm, and said,

"I'm sure they'll be sitting right where you left them when we get back." He swallowed down the lump of grief and anger in his throat.

"Do you want to stay here or go in?" He nodded toward the store entrance.

"Go," she said. She peeked under the cloth covering Baby's cage, seemed to find the bird okay, and unlatched her door and slid out into the rain.

A group of people stood under the front entrance awning, drinking coffee and smoking, and trading stories of their escapes. Disaster camaraderie. He'd seen a lot of that in the navy.

He and Phoebe wrung out the water from their clothes under the awning before entering the store. Inside more people huddled near the doors, drinking coffee, too, but silently as though being indoors made the situation more somber.

A few dozen other people wandered the aisles, eyes glazed over, staring at the goods. They were refugees in a land of mysterious objects. The glare of lights and the shiny floor gave Darren a slight headache.

Phoebe steered them away from the baby aisle, as she usually did, her hope to be a mother now an unspoken ache after the miscarriages. They shuffled along the bath products aisle. Phoebe pointed out things she liked—a peach colored soap set, silver-grey towels. Inside the windowless store, with its fluorescent brightness and cheer, they could be leisurely shopping on a Saturday afternoon. He watched the way she absent mindedly pushed her hair behind her ear. He suddenly wanted to touch the blond hairs on her tanned arms.

"Darren!" He turned in the aisle and saw his childhood friend Gerry, a large man with a shit-eating grin always plastered on his face. Gerry lumbered up to him and clapped him on the back. "You made it!"

"Barely," Darren said. "You remember Phoebe, right?"

Gerry nodded to Phoebe. "Ma'am. How does it look your way?"

Phoebe turned her head back to the towels to hide her crying. Gerry patted her on the shoulder. "Don't worry, Honey. It'll be okay."

"Just think, Pheeb," Darren said, half-heartedly joining Gerry's optimism, "Once the water's receded, I'll probably be busier than a squirrel in a nut factory with work orders."

"That's right," Gerry agreed. "They'll be lining up at your door for help drying out basements and cleaning up mold."

No longer hiding her weeping, Phoebe had pulled one of the silver-grey towels off the shelf and pressed it to her face.

It was late when the rain finally let up. On the radio the announcer said Nashville was under a couple feet of water. The announcers kept saying it was *historic* and *unprecedented.*

Phoebe slept, a towel cushioning her head against the window. He climbed down from the pickup and helped Mercy out so she could do her business, then lifted her into the back seat again.

Under the awning in front of Walmart, he lit a cigarette and listened to what people were saying about the local roads. Inside there was a television mounted near an exit door. A crowd of people in various stages of drying clothes looked up at it. But the news was airing shots only of Nashville.

He called his father, who was probably still up, glued to the television.

"The rain's stopped here," he said.

"Yup," his father answered, "here, too."

"I can't get any news on the radio. Except about Nashville."

"Well, shoot," his father said, joking. "That's all that counts, boy!"

"Huh," he answered and took another tug on his cigarette.

"Ten minutes ago, they said that Martin County was bad and they were sending out patrols to find people."

"Dang." That *was* bad news.

"Are you still at Walmart? Well, you should probably stay there for a while longer at least."

"That's what it's sounding like."

He was dying to get back to his place and see the damage. If they went back now and the bridge wasn't washed out, they could probably get there. But if the bridge was under? They'd have to turn back around. They couldn't leave the parking lot anyway without first asking ten other drivers to move their vehicles.

A Walmart greeter in a bright red smock was handing out free coffee. He thanked her and took the Styrofoam cup she gave him. He wished they were handing out free beers, but that wasn't going to happen in dry Martin County.

In the truck, he leaned his seat back and tried to sleep. It was past midnight, and he was exhausted, but sleep was a stranger so he cracked his window, lit another cigarette, and listened to WSM, the all-night country station out of Nashville.

By dawn Phoebe was awake and the parking lot held only about half the cars it did the night before. He hopped out of the truck, lifted Mercy down, let her relieve herself while Phoebe shook out some food into a plastic bowl. She poured a bottle of water into the other side of the bowl, which Mercy took a long drink of. Funny to be thirsty with all this rain, but there you were, animals had to be fed and watered, just like people.

Phoebe's phone rang. She looked at the caller ID and said, "Mama," before flipping the phone open to answer it.

While she talked he lit a cigarette for her.

"Pretty bad," she said into the phone. "But the rain's stopped, thank God."

He handed her the cigarette which she took with a wink to him.

"Yeah, but we had to leave yesterday . . . in the parking lot at Walmart . . . yeah, it weren't too bad. Got a bit of a neck kink."

He remembered the phone call that came in the middle of the night twenty years before when he was stationed in San Diego. The sergeant had shook him awake and he jerked upright. Then what his Dad said had scared him even more. At least no one was hurt. But the house was only the burnt shadow of itself—by the time the fire engines arrived they had all they could do to keep it from spreading to the neighbors.

His brother was still living with Dad then and he was shook up bad. It was an accident, an electrical wiring problem, the fire starting quietly in the wall while Dad and Tommy were sleeping. He wished he'd been there when the fire happened. He couldn't have done much, but still, it stank that he couldn't be there to help get more things out, like his mother's favorite chair and her quilts. Phoebe had been sad about that when he told her. "I wish I could have met her," she said. He wished that, too. All he had of her were a few grainy photos of her kneeling in the pasture fixing a fence, standing beside his father the day they were married, and her leaning over to present him with his first birthday cake.

There was a gap in the photos he had—he had those few of himself as a child when his mother was still alive, ones he had brought with him while in the navy, and he had pictures of his navy days, but his teen years had burned in the house fire.

When she had been real sick, dying in the hospital, he was granted some shore leave. Tommy was too young to visit at the hospital so he stood outside her window waving at their mother from the lawn. She took Darren's hand and squeezed it real hard, surprisingly hard for how weak she was from all the radiation and chemo. Sometimes he could still feel that squeeze, her way of saying *Keep on.*

In the store, Phoebe went to find breakfast. He hung around the television until there was a local story. It didn't look good. They had opened up Old Hickory to release the pressure from the lake water. The talking heads kept saying that if they hadn't opened the dam, it would have been even worse than it was in Nashville. Closer to home, roads were still washed out and emergency workers were looking for the stranded by helicopter and boat.

Phoebe returned with Cokes and a package of donuts. Wiry and muscular, he could still eat like a teenager and get away with it.

They decided to see how far they could get, despite the warnings that the river was continuing to rise. Maybe they'd have to turn around and come back. But he couldn't just sit in the parking lot anymore doing nothing.

The first few miles out on the county highway everything looked fine. He had to navigate the pickup around a few tree limbs, but otherwise, the sun was already drying up the surrounding fields and roads. As they got closer to the river, he started to see double-wides tipped off their foundations and trucks in the middle of fields where the water still stood a few inches deep.

The bridge was under water.

He knew they should turn back. If the river was this high, the water would have already engulfed the basement, maybe even the first floor.

The sky was cloudless and the sun reflected off the water. Birds twittered in the trees. A perfect day for a float on the river.

Phoebe's face was wet with tears. "Nature's gone beserk. I'm telling you, it's a sign," she said. "The Man upstairs is trying to tell us something."

Maybe Phoebe was right. He'd heard talk of more frequent floods to come. The future of extreme weather. It sounded as though disaster was the new normal.

"I can take drought," she said. "But this?"

He looked at the swollen river. A red door floated by, followed by tires, a bright yellow plastic slide, cans and big chunks of Styrofoam, a chair, and so many branches they piled up at the sides of the bridge, clogging the railings.

He reached into the backseat and got out the hip waders he always kept stored in the truck and changed out of his work boots. He wasn't going to risk ruining a pair of his most expensive boots.

Mercy lifted her head from the arm rest and looked out the window then back at him.

"Yes, sweetheart, we have to stop here. Don't ya worry. I'll come back for you." He left the windows halfway down.

"*We*'ll come back for you," Phoebe said, crushing her cigarette in the ashtray.

"But I only have one pair of waders," he protested.

She shrugged.

"It's not safe. You don't know what's in that water," he said.

"Then it's not safe for you neither."

He took the waders off and gave them to her and then changed into a pair of old sneakers he dug out of one of the storage containers.

He unstrapped the kayaks and lifted them down. He placed them just at the water's edge. Then he handed Phoebe an oar. They paddled their way across the bridge.

A small trailer perched in the branches of trees along the river bank. A washing machine bobbed nearby. A man's red dress shirt clung to a bush like a headless scarecrow.

The road was submerged but they followed the line of trees.

He saw Jimmy's place first, or, that is, he didn't see it. Only the flat roof of Jimmy's ramshackle trailer was visible above the murky brown water. There was no sign of Jimmy.

Darren screwed his eyes shut. "Lord, have mercy," he whispered. He opened his eyes and looked toward their house.

The river was all the way up to the windows, and he could see that the water mark was even higher, a mucky black line of silt a foot or so above the water. The photos would be ruined.

The van had floated across the road into a neighbor's field. There, the water was not nearly as high, dissuaded by the field's gentle slope.

The kayaks knocked against the house as though tethered to a dock. Phoebe finished her cigarette, crushing it against a roof shingle and then flicking it into the water.

"Yep," she sighed. "The signs are clear."

Just then they heard the geese braying from the other side of the house. He lifted his head to greet the birds, but instead startled at the sound of a gunshot. Darren flung out his arms and smacked them flat against the roof. Phoebe flinched and crouched down.

The geese honked and sputtered, flapping their wings. Darren peeked over the roof's midline.

Across the water Jimmy cackled from the roof of his trailer, wearing an orange shirt and waving his shotgun at Darren.

"Didn't see ya there!"

"You could have killed us, you bastard!"

"Terrible sorry," Jimmy said, then chuckled. He was drunk.

The geese looked okay, none hurt. They glided away from the house, bobbing and weaving around each other, murmuring quiet notes of comfort.

Phoebe stood up and yelled across the expanse. "You're one sorry motherfucker, ya know?"

"I know!"

Darren shook his head. "What do you do with someone like that?"

"I don't know," Phoebe said, "but I also don't know how he's going to get off his house."

Darren looked over at the man. The trailer roof was flat but slanted with one end submerged.

"I have a mind to leave him there," Darren said. "We can call rescue when we get back to the highway."

"It's supposed to get worse."

He frowned. She was right. They had to help the bastard, even if he had tried to shoot the geese. Even if the guy was one more reason Phoebe would leave.

"Where do you think Amber and Cat are?" she asked, twisting around to take in the tree line.

Unless they were in one of those trees, he knew they were gone. But he didn't say it.

"We gotta look," Phoebe said, crawling over to the side of the roof the kayaks were tied to.

They lowered themselves into the kayaks and paddled to the closest tree, the two of them calling, "Here, puss puss! Here, puss puss!"

After several minutes, and having checked six trees, they heard a faint mewing sound from near the van. They paddled over to the water's edge in the meadow and pulled the kayaks up. There in a patch of wet grass Amber delicately stepped towards them. Phoebe scooped her up and held the cat's matted gray and white body against her chest. "Where's Cat?" she asked Amber. "Where's your buddy?" Amber purred loudly.

Darren looked back at the house. The farmer who owned this meadow talked about selling a couple years ago. Maybe Darren would put an offer down. If the farmer accepted, then Darren could move up to drier land. Maybe then the insurance company would give him flood coverage.

With Amber in Phoebe's kayak, they paddled back to the pickup. He left Phoebe there with the animals and paddled back through the yellow-brown water to Jimmy with the second kayak tied behind his. It was eerie how quiet it was. No motors from the highway. Just a rustle of wind in the trees and the soft slap of his paddles in the water.

Jimmy lay flat on his back, but he must have heard Darren's approach because he sat up when Darren was only a few feet away.

"It's my house," Jimmy said to him, as though there were some dispute about it.

Darren brought the kayak up alongside the edge of the trailer.

"The river seems to think differently," he said. There was a powerful smell coming off of Jimmy. The man had a few days of beard growth and his graying hair was flattened across his forehead. His low-riding pants and orange t-shirt were smudged with what looked like engine grease. He was missing a boot. The rifle lay to the side of his leg.

"I'm not leaving."

"Don't be a fool, Jimmy," Darren said. "It's not safe. They're saying the river will keep on rising for a day or so."

Jimmy looked at him, his eyes unfocused, considering.

"C'mon, man," Darren said. "We gotta go."

Jimmy reached behind him and Darren tensed, gripping his paddle tighter in case he needed to use it. The crazy fool pulled out a couple of beers hanging from a six-pack ring.

"Want one?" He held a corner of the ring and waved the beers at Darren.

"Shit, man! Save 'em for when we get to the truck."

Jimmy aimed the beers at the empty kayak and let go. The beers dropped and rolled into the water. Jimmy pitched forward, reaching for them, and nearly fell. The beers floated for a second, then sank.

"Damn, why didn't you save them?" Jimmy demanded, angry now.

"Because I'm trying to save you, you bastard!"

"Fuck," Jimmy said, and for a moment Darren thought the man was still contemplating going in after the beers.

Jimmy noticed his unpaired boot and untied it and threw it in the water. "Won't be needing that, I reckon."

"Nope. Just the bare necessities."

"Me and my gun." Jimmy grinned, revealing a missing front tooth.

With much grunting, Jimmy repositioned himself on all fours and crawled to the edge of the trailer, dragging his rifle alongside him. He hesitated, unsure how to get in. Darren gripped the empty kayak to steady it.

"C'mon," Darren said, nodding his head, since he didn't have a free hand. "Get in."

The man aligned himself along the length of the kayak and shuffled his knees closer to the edge, then backed one leg in.

The kayak rocked and Darren tried to settle it. "Slow and steady," he said. Jimmy leaned his weight into the kayak and rolled right over it into Darren, knocking them both in the water.

For a moment Darren didn't know which way was up as Jimmy thrashed about and the kayaks banged into him. Just as his head broke the surface and he gulped air, he felt the flailing weight of Jimmy's arm come down hard on his shoulder. He tried to grab for it but Jimmy was panicked and wouldn't stop moving.

Darren tried to grab anything he could and realized he was still gripping the paddle. He opened his mouth to shout to Jimmy but the water sloshed around him and he swallowed the murky river instead.

Then Darren saw the flash of the kayak's yellow body near him and he reached for it, flipping it over on top of him. He swam out from under it and then grasped his arm around one end where the kayak narrowed. With the other arm, still holding the paddle, he searched the water for Jimmy. "Jimmy!" The scream came out as a sputter.

He put his head underwater and opened his eyes, but the river was so clouded he couldn't see even as far as his own hand.

Raising his head to breathe, he tried to think quickly. He lifted the paddle up and back, winding up his arm to throw the paddle on the trailer. Then he used his free hand to swim to the roof. There he steadied himself, gripped the kayak rope in his teeth, and hauled himself over the edge of the trailer.

He scanned the waters again. He shouted Jimmy's name, his hoarse voice echoing off the far bank of the river. He had thought he could help Jimmy. Darren hadn't saved much else, but he thought he could at least save that fool of a neighbor. Though, heaven knew, the man had a death wish. But, Jesus, he just couldn't fail at this.

He squinted in the sun, watching for ripples and eddies for what felt like hours but surely was only minutes.

Reluctantly, he lowered himself back into the kayak and let the current take him, steadying the boat when the river threatened to spin him or crash him into a tree.

No Jimmy. The bridge came into view. And the truck, where Mercy lollygagged her head out the driver's side window, looking at Phoebe who stood in the waders, one hand on the truck door, a cigarette in the other. The water lapped at Phoebe's ankles but she didn't seem to notice, her face tilted up toward the sun.

He raised his paddle and hollered. Phoebe turned to see him but the river had already shot him over the bridge, hurrying him and everything else it scooped up as far as it could go.

The Corner Cupboard

I think I'm slowly turning into my first landlady. When I knew her, she was in her 40s, approximately the same age I am now, short and stocky with blonde hair set in a bouffant style. I didn't see her that often, but her physical presence wasn't necessary for her to nonetheless loom large in my life.

It was my first year of grad school. Three other grad students and I shared the first floor of a brick A-frame in a small college town in western Massachusetts. Lincoln Avenue was a wide tree-lined street that bordered the university campus. Since I was the last one to answer the ad, I got the smallest bedroom, off the kitchen, just enough space for a single bed and desk.

Four undergraduate women occupied the second floor. They blasted their music and watched television on loud. When we called to ask them to turn down the volume, they'd turn it up and stomp overhead.

So, yeah, the undergrads upstairs were class-A bitches.

But the landlady. She existed on her own plane of bitchness. If there were a Bitch Olympics, she'd qualify instantly, win the gold.

The kitchen, dining area, and living room were on an open

floor plan. Except that there was a corner cupboard, floor to ceiling, set between the dining room and the kitchen. It was a *corner* cupboard, a 3-D triangle. Like the triangular blocks that preschoolers shove into square and round holes in a brightly colored box to learn their geometric shapes. Such toys created generations of frustrated children who grew up to become frustrated adults, like my landlady.

The *corner* cupboard was not anywhere near one of the corners. It stood silent and loomed like a giant sentry, a useless Beefeater.

If I was sitting at the dining table, eating or writing a paper, and I wanted to go to my room, which would have otherwise been a quick hop and jump on a straight diagonal, I had to skirt around the cupboard. Toes were stubbed, curses muttered.

To add insult to injury, there was a gap between the cupboard and a narrow wall on the other side of which sat the stove. So, conceivably, one could set a cupboard against *that* wall, a regular rectangular cupboard or shelf. But, no. That idea was too logical. No, there was a *corner* cupboard and it was not even flush with the wall, hence the unusable space between the wall and the pointy back edge of the cupboard.

At this point in our relationships, my housemates and I were four strangers eager to start off on the right foot. We were studying in different programs—English (me), Communications, Speech Pathology, and International Studies—and probably above average in intelligence and generally reasonable. We all had our quirks. I tended to keep to myself. Elena, the speech pathologist, spoke, strangely enough, at a volume that hurt my ears sometimes. Cassie was part Colombian and liked dangly earrings. The Communications student, Jen, was the only second-year grad student and tended toward bossy. She took command of our house meetings. At the first meeting, she suggested we move the cupboard to where we all—as generally reasonable people—agreed it belonged: in the corner.

Cassie took down the dusty bowl and miniature wood plow that served as decoration on the cupboard shelves and set them on the dining table. Elena and I awkwardly grasped the cupboard, finding some leverage with our hands under the first shelf, and moved it to a far corner of the dining room, where it fit snugly and had a full view of the entire common area (if the cupboard had been endowed with eyes).

With a dish rag, Cassie dusted the decorative objects and replaced them on the shelves.

And we were done. Everything seemed to be in its place.

Orientations and classes started. We adjusted to each other's schedules. Cassie was gone all the time, from early in the morning until sometimes well after I was in bed. I was probably home the most, since our house was on the edge of campus and thus a five-minute walk from the building where I took courses and taught first-year comp. But Elena and Jen were in and out, too, at random times.

One day, probably a week or two after our first house meeting, I came home from class and Elena was standing in the kitchen talking on the house phone. She acknowledged me with a slight shift in her posture. Her eyes were directed up in that unfocused way people have when talking on the phone and she repeated "Uh huh. Okay" several times in her loud, clear soprano.

When she hung up, she stepped into the living room where I was. "You'll never believe what that was about."

"What?"

"Mrs. Deetz wants us to move the corner cupboard back."

"What?" It took me a moment to process what Elena was saying. I glanced at the cupboard, nestled happily in its corner, as though looking at the actual object would aid my understanding.

"Yeah, it's crazy. With a capital 'C.' She said, 'the terms of your lease stipulate you cannot move furniture.'" Elena mimicked the high-pitched, nasal voice of our landlady while wagging her head churlishly.

Jen emerged from her basement bedroom with a bowl and spoon in hand. She licked the spoon and held it up for our inspection. "Ice cream," she explained and put the dishes in the sink. She peeked around the stove. "*Who* cannot move furniture?"

"You won't believe it," I said, and then blushed at how excited I sounded.

"I just got off the phone with Mrs. Deetz," Elena said.

"Oh?"

I jumped in, still unable to contain myself. "She wants us to move the cupboard back to its original spot."

Jen looked puzzled.

"Yup," Elena said. "That's what *I* thought too."

"But how did she . . . ?" Jen started to ask and then opened her eyes wide. "Did she come in the house? She can't do that, you know, without giving us notice."

"She said that she came by this morning to mow the lawn and saw through the window that the cupboard had been moved."

"That's creepy," Jen said. I nodded vigorously in agreement. I didn't remember hearing the sound of the mower, but I also was a late sleeper.

I hadn't always been a late riser. But in Pittsburgh the previous summer, I had waited tables, and working almost to midnight every night readjusted my sleep schedule. It also had caused some friction with my boyfriend. We were relatively new to each other, had dated for a few months and then moved in together the summer before I applied to grad school. Trevor was an analyst for an investment company downtown. Made buttloads. But long hours, up at the crack, home after dark. Once I took the waiting job, we hardly saw each other.

Trevor liked to joke—though I don't think he was completely joking—that I didn't need to work, I could be a kept woman. When I told him I was going to grad school in Massachusetts, he was happy for me, but I could also sense he was worried about "us."

"What if we refuse to move it?" Jen asked.

"She said if we don't move it she'll come in and move it herself," Elena said.

"You think she'd do that?" I said.

Jen shrugged. "Let's see what Cassie says."

That night when Cassie finally got home, we held another house meeting. The girls upstairs were playing Phish at record-high decibels. I had been under the impression, apparently false, that the people who went to Phish concerts were hippies, not mean girls.

"Least they could play something decent," Cassie said, her dark brown eyes lively with laughter. Fabric women in brightly colored poofy folk skirts danced at the end of her ears.

"Exactly," Jen agreed.

"So, Mrs. Deetz is spying on us?" Cassie asked, plunging her hand into a bag of potato chips. She pulled out a large chip which she crunched loudly before offering the bag around.

"Weird, eh?" Jen sometimes used Canadian inflections because she had spent the summer in Banff.

"She said she just *happened* to see that the cupboard was moved," Elena said, speaking in an exaggeratingly formal manner.

"That early in the morning without lights on in the house," I said, "she'd have to come up to the window and press her face against the glass to see anything inside."

"Like I said. *Weird.*" Jen flapped her spoon in the air. She was eating ice cream again.

"So, what do you think? Should we move it back?" I asked Cassie.

Cassie chewed on her lips and then looked coy. "I say let's do nothing and see . . ."

"What?" The music upstairs had abruptly increased in volume and Elena was covering her ears and shouting at the same time.

Jen set her ice cream bowl down with a clatter, then jumped up and grabbed the broom from the kitchen. Holding the bristle end, she knocked the handle against the ceiling. The floorboards stopped squeaking. We'd at least gotten their attention but the music continued to blare. Jen knocked a couple more times.

For a moment, nothing changed. Then the girls upstairs stomped and jumped around and the ceiling shuddered above our heads, upping the ante.

"Fuck this shit!" Elena yelled. She lunged at the phone and dialed. The rest of us waited while Elena listened for someone to pick up. Jen still held the broom aloft, positioned to knock more, if necessary.

A minute went by while we waited. Then Elena slammed the receiver. "They won't answer, the little shits!"

Jen set the broom against the wall and headed toward the door.

"I gotta see this!" Cassie said, following Jen.

Elena and I ran to the side window where, outside, first Jen and then Cassie passed on their way to the stairs to the second-floor apartment. After a few seconds, the music cut out and we could hear voices.

"Sorry! We didn't hear you."

A door slammed. Feet clomped down the stairs.

When they came back inside, Jen was grinning and Cassie was frowning. The music upstairs came on again at full blast, making us all freeze in surprise and disbelief, but then the volume lowered again such that only the dull thud of the drums were discernible.

Elena let out a loud sigh and rolled her eyes. "What is their freakin' problem?"

"I've barely said two words to them since we met," I said. "Why do they hate us?"

Jen threw herself onto the couch. "The one—with long dark hair—I can't remember her name—when I told her the music was too loud, she acted as though she had no idea."

"The others all hid in their rooms." Cassie crossed to the recliner in the corner and plopped down. She picked up the bag of chips. "Anyway, we were saying?"

"The cupboard," I prompted.

"Oh, yeah! I say we just ignore Mrs. Deetz and not do a thing," Cassie said.

We looked at each other. If we had felt peeved before about our landlady's strange obsession about the corner cupboard, the skirmish with the undergrads upstairs made us boldly disobedient. Disobedience wasn't my strong suit. I was both excited and anxious about the prospect of this passive declaration of war.

That week I faced my first pile of composition papers to grade, topic: "Describe a significant place in your life." Trevor hadn't answered my last couple of phone calls. When I finally got him on the phone, he mumbled about work being crazy, having to wine and dine clients, late nights, early mornings. He seemed only vaguely interested when I recounted my adventures in group housing and teaching woes (students who didn't show up for appointments, having to share a desk with another grad student in a former psychology lab in the basement, complete with one-way mirrors).

One day after class I was walking home with an armful of papers to grade. It was hot in that way it gets in New England in autumn, a last gasp of summer humidity before the cold sets in. My students had been listless. My hair was both frizzed out and plastered to my skull. I was looking forward to a cool shower and a glass of wine before facing more essays about beaches and grandparents' backyards.

I fumbled for my key at the door. It was a cute door, the top rounded until it came to a point, one you might imagine adorning the grandmother's house in "Red Riding Hood."

The papers I held were slipping out of my grasp. I left the key in the door and shuffled quickly to the dining table where the papers fell into a disheveled mess. As I stood over the table, I noticed two things at once: how quiet the house was—I must have been the only one home unless someone was napping or studying—and that something was not quite right. A strange sensation crept over me and it took me a moment to realize that my body was oriented differently than usual to the objects around me.

The corner cupboard was back in its original location, standing sentry between the dining room and kitchen.

I stared at it, walked all the way around it to be sure I wasn't hallucinating.

Despite the heat, goosebumps broke out on my arms and legs and I felt chilled. I moved quickly to the front windows and peeked outside. Both yard and street were empty. I ran to the windows skirting the driveway. No cars there. The neighbors, also grad students, were playing a lazy game of Frisbee in their yard, but no one was near our house.

I crossed the room to the hallway and knocked on Cassie's door. No answer. Elena's room door was open, how she usually left it when she was out. I knocked on Jen's basement room door but there was no reply there either.

My heart thumped hard in my chest. The goosebumps had vanished and now I was sweating. I tried to remind myself that nothing sinister had happened. Mrs. Deetz had simply entered the apartment and moved the cupboard. Then I thought of my room. Would she have gone in there? It was a mess, dirty clothes on the floor, the bed unmade, papers and books everywhere.

I checked. Everything was as I had left it. But I had no way of knowing if the landlady had looked in my room or not. It wasn't as though I had been doing anything illegal. There was nothing in the lease that said I had to keep my room tidy. Of the four housemates, Elena was the neatest—though she left dirty dishes in the sink a lot—but I didn't think I'd be crowned the most slovenly.

I thought about calling Trevor, but long distance calls would still be on daytime rates at that hour, before five o'clock.

Instead, I collected myself, retrieved my key, shut the front door, neatly stacked the papers, and went to take a shower.

The cool water was divine. I found myself singing, "Pack up all your troubles in your old kit bag, and smile, smile, smile," which my mother used to drive me crazy humming all the time.

As I was toweling dry, I heard someone moving around in the kitchen. Jen was rummaging in the fridge when I came out from the bathroom. She looked at me over the fridge door.

"Can you believe it?" she said, closing the door.

I shook my head. My earlier fear had now settled into a pleasant frisson of excitement. Our landlady was a nut and we were all bonding as a result!

"Why do you think she cares so much about the cupboard?"

"A control freak. Her husband used to be a psychology professor," Jen said. "They own a dozen properties in town, and they're always in court for some reason."

"How do you know?"

"The local paper. And you know the house around the corner? Like three stories and probably twenty undergrads?" I nodded. "One of them is in my Intro to Communications class and Mrs. Deetz is charging her and her housemates for the thumbtack holes in the walls. The tenants are contesting the charge."

I was reminded of my suitcase gouging the bedroom wall when I moved in. I'd have to get some spackle and paint to cover it up.

"Help me move it back?" Jen pointed at the cupboard.

"Don't you think we should leave it?"

"Oh, come on. You're not going to give in that easy, are you?"

"Let's talk to Elena and Cassie first."

"Suit yourself." Jen shrugged and went to the basement.

That night Elena and Cassie were incensed. Cassie stormed around the house, green hummingbird earrings shaking and spinning. "I can't believe her! What is her problem?"

"I say we move it back." Jen was standing in the living room, hands on hips, ready for action.

"Yes!" Cassie agreed. The two of them picked up the cupboard and shuffled it over to the corner. Elena stood aside, holding the decorative bowl and plow until the cupboard was in place. I realized I was chewing my cuticles and put my hands in my pockets.

"Shouldn't we put curtains up or something?" I meekly offered. "She'll just come snooping again."

"Does anyone know how to sew?" Elena asked. The last time I had looked at a sewing machine, the needle instantly broke. "Plus none of us has a sewing machine."

A couple days later I returned home to find Jen and Elena standing in the dining room talking spiritedly. "Maggie! Look!" Elena flung her arm out, leading my gaze to where the cupboard stood once again in no man's land between dining room and kitchen.

I blinked at it. I was only 25 but I was beginning to grasp a certain truth: No matter how trivial the competition, humans hate to lose.

"*And* did you notice?" Jen asked Elena.

"What?"

"It's screwed down."

"What?!"

Jen beckoned us forward to the cupboard where she placed a hand on its side and pushed on the offending piece of furniture as though she meant to topple it. But it was so securely attached to the floor no amount of pushing would budge it.

I opened the doors to the bottom shelves, which were empty except for eight shiny new screws embedded in the floor panel and bits of wood shavings.

Leaning back on my heels, I said, with exaggerated finality, "I guess she doesn't want us to move the cupboard."

It wasn't as though I was new to nutty behavior. There was always plenty of crazy to go around in my extended family, a grandfather who skipped out on his wife for years while he was drunk and homeless, an aunt who was institutionalized for depression. But while there was some eccentricity in my immediate family—if you opened kitchen drawers you might find one crammed with wine corks and another with rubber bands— it didn't extend to nailing down random pieces of furniture for no explicable reason. In houses we didn't even live in ourselves no less.

When I called Trevor that night, he didn't pick up. I left a brief, cryptic message, hoping to entice him to return my call. "More landlady news. She moved the cupboard again. And there's more. Call me back. Love you."

Around 9:30 Cassie returned home and we decided that Mrs. Deetz should get a phone call. After a bit of discussion, Elena was persuaded to make the call since she had already emerged as a natural spokeswoman. I felt relieved that it wouldn't be me.

Elena stood as far as the phone cord would let her into the living area, her eyes directed at the ceiling while she waited for Mrs. Deetz to pick up. I realized I was holding my breath and let it out in a slow exhale. I had started taking a yoga class on Tuesdays and Thursdays. The instructor had told the students to pay attention to our breathing, which I had thought was a little funny at first because breathing was involuntary. But I was beginning to understand what she meant.

"Mrs. Deetz?" Elena's voice struck a higher than usual note. "It's Elena at 314 Lincoln? My . . . I'm fine, thank you." Elena made crazy eyes at us, impatient to get to the point. "My housemates and I noticed that the cupboard we spoke about the other day? It's been nailed to the floor. . . . Yes, I *know* . . . but . . . see, we never got notice, did we?" Elena extended her head, directing the question at us. We shook our heads. "No, none of us got that message. Okay, but . . . but why is a *corner* cupboard in the middle of the room?" Elena listened intently to the response.

"Okay, then, let's talk about the stove," Elena said and pivoted sharply and walked into the kitchen. "We called the manufacturer. The last time this model was made was in 1972. . . . Yup. And when we complained that the back burners didn't work you told us the stove was only five years old. Yet you send someone in to nail the corner cupboard to the floor?"

Cassie, Jen, and I glanced at each other, impressed with Elena's quick thinking. I hardly cooked, subsisting mostly on ramen noodles, cereal, and apples, so I had forgotten about the burners not working.

"Oh, I see," said Elena. "But you *lied* to us."

The rest of the conversation lasted only a minute or so and mostly consisted of Elena nodding and saying "Okay" a million times.

When she hung up, the rest of us could barely contain our eagerness to hear what Mrs. Deetz had said.

Elena strode into the living room and clapped her hands together in mock satisfaction. "So. She won't move the corner cupboard. *But—*" Elena held a finger up, as though she were arguing a dramatic case in a court room—"she is going to replace the stove."

"Well, that's *something* at least," Cassie said, getting up. "I have tons of reading for tomorrow."

"I wouldn't hold your breath," Jen said, taking her ice cream bowl into the kitchen. "But, good work, Elena!"

"Yes," I chimed in. "You could be a lawyer."

Elena beamed at us and then bounced off to her room, no doubt to call her friend Brianna. For the next two hours, while I read about shimmering waves and hot sand, childhood swing sets, and pink-curtained bedrooms, I could hear Elena's voice through the walls. When I finally closed my eyes to sleep, her melodic chirp was still ringing in my ears.

For Columbus Day weekend the four of us scattered, me to visit Trevor in Pittsburgh, Cassie to stay with a friend in Brooklyn, Jen to her family in upstate New York, and Elena to Boston. I got back to the house late Monday night, the last one to return. There was a lamp on in the living room, giving off a soft glow and soothing piano music coming from behind Elena's door. When I stepped inside, my body felt more relaxed than it had been all weekend. Trevor had been distant the whole time, even when we were in bed. He seemed to be going through the motions. I hadn't realized it, though, until walking in the door at Lincoln Avenue.

Cassie was talking on the phone. She waved and raised her index finger to indicate I should wait until she was done. She said her goodbyes to whoever it was and put down the phone.

"How's it going?" she said, sidling up to me. I could tell she had something to tell me.

"Fine. And you?"

"Good. Guess what."

"Mrs. Deetz has finally come to her senses about the cupboard."

Cassie snorted and did a little skipping step over to the dining table. "Hardly. Look at this." She held up a piece of paper. I saw right away that it was on a fancy linen stock with the return address embossed in gold at the top. *Mrs. Arianna Deetz.* I had forgotten that Mrs. Deetz had a first name. Of course she did, but *Arianna* struck me as too elegant for the woman who snooped around her tenants' windows and nailed down wooden objects.

After the salutation, the letter read:

> Your lease explicitly states that you may not move furniture at 314 Lincoln Avenue. If one or more of you attempt to move furniture again, I will serve you with an eviction notice. Consider this letter to be your only warning.
>
> Sincerely,
> Arianna Deetz

"Can she do that? Evict us like that?" I asked.

Cassie took the letter from me and folded it back into its envelope. "Jen says she can't. That Massachusetts law favors tenants."

Somehow that didn't reassure me. The rent was $300 a month and if we got evicted I'd lose $600 in security and last month's rent. But it was only a warning, and I had no intention of moving anything bigger than a cooking pot.

The semester's work was piling on and I spent my time either in class or in my room studying and grading. On Halloween, the four of us had dinner together and listened to the girls upstairs hopping around getting ready to go out. The music was blasting and there was a lot of squealing, but, hey, we weren't total wet blankets so we let them have their ghoulish fun.

When the music stopped and we heard the undergrads clomping down the stairs, we turned the lights off and spied on them through the windows. They were dressed in various skimpy black clothes, which made them hard to see. "Cats?" Elena wondered.

A little later, Elena went to a party with Brianna, and Cassie met up with her International Studies friends. Jen disappeared into her basement room to talk with her boyfriend on the extension down there.

I decided to take a walk and threw on my jean jacket, having yet to invest in a winter coat. My legs started shivering within a couple minutes as I kicked the fallen leaves around outside. There were no street lamps until the road met the university campus a few hundred yards down the street. I stood for a moment, waiting for my eyes to adjust to the dark. The stars gradually faded in to view. Having lived in cities all my life—Washington, D.C. then Pittsburgh—the night sky was still exotic. For a moment I reveled in the realization of our tiny, fleeting human existence. How bizarre that we existed at all.

From down the street there came a loud whooping. A mob of undergrads was making its way toward the house. I ran back inside, telling myself I wasn't dressed for the weather anyway.

For the rest of the evening, I listened to hordes of students who wandered up and down the street, shouting, drinking, flinging beer bottles into yards. I drifted off to sleep around one a.m. reading *Frankenstein* and wondering whether Trevor was at the costume party he said he might go to and who he was meeting.

A couple weeks before Thanksgiving, Trevor and I had our first real fight. He was going to his parents' house in Ohio for the holiday and thought I should go alone to my mother's house. Divorced since forever, my mother still lived in D.C. and my father had moved to the west coast. I had thought Trevor was coming with me to visit my mother but he had changed his mind, and I couldn't very well leave my mother by herself for Thanksgiving.

I hung up still annoyed at the conversation with Trevor, and when I returned the phone to the kitchen, Cassie was standing there holding one of those notices UPS leaves on your doorknob when you're not at home.

"Did a package get delivered for me?" she asked. Today she wore big silver hoops that jingle-jangled with every movement she made.

"I don't think so," I said. "At least I didn't see one. Maybe they rang the bell and I didn't hear it 'cause I was on the phone?"

"Maybe," she said. "It would have been a big package and this says that it was delivered to the back door. I checked, nothing's there."

"That's strange," I said, but as I spoke I realized what must have happened. I pointed upstairs.

"Do you think they'd stoop that low?" Cassie said, narrowing her eyes. "It was a vacuum cleaner. For my mom. What would they want with it?"

"To complete their mean girl certification course?"

Cassie crossed back to the phone. I put some water on the stove for tea, mostly so I had a reason to hang around and see what happened.

"Hello? Hi, this is Cassie. From downstairs? Yeah. Uhm, did anyone on your floor see a package? UPS delivered it. A big one." After a few seconds, Cassie said, "Okay. Can you ask your roommates? All right. Thanks."

The water boiled and I poured it in a mug.

"Well," Cassie said, sighing. "At least it's insured." And it was. Cassie was able to order another one and this time UPS delivered it when someone was home and we just threw up our hands at the mysterious disappearance of the first vacuum.

A week later, on a Wednesday night, it was a little after dinner time and the usual tomfoolery was happening upstairs, music blasting, squealing, stomping. As the semester wore on, the partying started earlier and earlier in the week. But we were grad students. We had pages to read and write, papers to grade, fellowship applications due.

We were cleaning up from dinner, hanging around, waiting for the party girls to clear out. After a few minutes we heard them coming down the stairs, but the music continued. I hadn't noticed at first. Then Elena said, "Are they gone?"

We listened for the sounds of bodies moving. But there was only the thump of bass and percussion that shook the ceiling on a regular beat.

"They fucking left the music on!" Elena yelled. "Bastards."

I started to giggle. I couldn't help it. The laughter snaked up my throat and burst me open.

Trevor was probably breaking up with me. I had so much work to do it freaked me out, and I had skipped yoga class that week, so my stress was pent up. And it was all too much.

"What? What?" Cassie came out from the kitchen, wiping her hands on a dish towel. "What's so funny?" She had to yell to be heard over the music.

Jen shut the faucet off and joined us. Now I was bent over and laughing so hard I was crying. "Tell us!" Cassie said, starting to laugh herself.

I waved at Elena. "You . . . ," I said, but that's all I could get out. My stomach ached.

Elena turned to Cassie and Jen. "They left the house but didn't shut off their fucking music!"

I was starting to be able to breathe again. They were short, shallow breaths, but at least there was some oxygen involved.

Cassie threw the dish towel on the table. "That's it! *This is war.*" She walked to the front door, threw it open, and marched out. Jen, Elena, and I looked at each other for a beat, then scrambled to follow her.

Cassie was already at the top of the stairs, knocking and peering through the four little panes of glass on the door. She put her hand to the doorknob and turned. Much to her surprise and ours—we had reached the landing where she stood—the door was unlocked.

We crowded into the entrance of the apartment, taking in the sight. Cereal bowls and plates sat askew on the coffee table competing for surfaces with magazines and videotapes. The grey console of a PlayStation peeked out between cushions on the couch. Clothes were flung about furniture and floor.

Jen crossed purposely to the stereo and flicked the volume down. "Well, well, well," she said, examining the chaos.

"I'm going to find that vacuum." Cassie began to walk the perimeter of the room, stepping over clothes, CD cases, books, empty soda cans.

"Doesn't look like they know how to use one," I said. Seeing the state of the undergrads' place made me feel less embarrassed about my bedroom mess.

I watched Jen look behind the table where the stereo and TV sat. "What are you doing?" I said and got closer.

"Crossing wires," she said, chuckling.

"Good Lord!" Elena said gleefully and jumped in beside Jen.

I stood there, chewing on my fingernail and glancing back at the door. What if they came in now? We were breaking and entering, weren't we?

Cassie skirted the last corner of the room and went into the hallway. "Jesus!" she called back. "This place is a mess!" I followed her. The floor layout was a little different from our apartment. The bedrooms flanked the hall, two on each side, with the bathroom at the very end.

I peeked in the first bedroom. I couldn't tell where the bed was because blankets and clothes were piled high, covering the entire room.

"Found it!" Cassie's voice was followed by dull bumping and thudding in the next bedroom.

When I stepped back into the hallway, she was lugging out the vacuum. "Ha!" She held up the nozzle in the air triumphantly.

I followed her back into the main room. Jen and Elena were still focused on unplugging and re-plugging the audio-visual cables. I looked down and spied a remote control on the couch. It was a petty idea and the undergrads deserved much, much worse. But I grabbed the remote and went into the kitchen.

The sink and counters were filled with dishes encrusted with food. A long drip of red sauce had dried on the front of the oven. The microwave door was hanging open, exposing its splattered interior. I closed it, then started to open drawers randomly, trying to find the junk drawer.

There didn't seem to be a drawer dedicated to junk—probably because the entire apartment was trashed—so I chose the drawer with cooking utensils and oven mitts and shoved the remote as far back into it as possible.

I felt a rush of adrenaline. Laughter pushed up out of my throat again. Clasping a hand over my mouth, I hopped into the main room.

"What'd ya do?" Cassie asked, grinning at me.

I let the laughter loose. Then after a minute I caught my breath and told her.

"That's perfect!" Jen said, popping up from behind the table. Her approval gave me another surge of joy. She brushed her hands together and said, "I think our work here is done."

We giggled and whooped our way down the stairs, descending back into our grad school lives.

We never heard a thing afterwards. Thanksgiving came, then winter break. Our revenge had been swift and improvised, and, except for the vacuum, there was no evidence of our transgression. I knew the girls upstairs couldn't complain, even though they must have known it was us. How would they explain the vacuum?

The silence was oddly disappointing. We had crossed a line, misbehaved and trespassed. And yet, without a response, it was as though nothing had happened.

All this occurred more than two decades ago. Now I live in my own house, a town over from Lincoln Avenue. I don't know if Mrs. Deetz is still alive, and I've lost touch with my partners in crime.

I married Craig, a man I met in my yoga class that spring of my first year in grad school. Our daughter is upstairs now, calming down after an argument we had about loading the dishwasher. Plastics need to be *handwashed*. In saying that to my daughter, I was suddenly taken back twenty years, my previous self dusted off like a forgotten gee-gaw on a shelf.

The AC hums in the corner. The summer has been brutal but the afternoon storm yesterday brought some of the yard back to life. I can hear the muted grumble of Craig mowing the lawn.

I've set my alarm to wake us all tonight at two a.m. in hopes we'll see the Perseids meteor shower. We'll crane our necks to look up at the dark sky dotted with distant suns, their light an echo of a memory, and stake our feeble claim in the universe.

Intruder

The trouble had started a year ago, in small ways: a neighbor's passing without even a nod to her in church; a tense hush when she walked by the trading post; Mrs. North no longer calling at the house. These gestures were rumblings, seismic shivers only, compared to her husband's dismissal, and then the troubles this week.

Monday morning she had gone out to collect eggs and nearly fell over one of her hens lying just outside the door, its neck twisted.

That same night she was startled awake by thudding on the roof. She reached in the dark to light a candle and checked that both boys were asleep in their beds before tiptoeing into the front room. There she stood for a moment listening to what sounded like hailstones falling but they came in single thuds, not many at once as had occurred in August when a nor'easter blew through and took out several panes.

She pinched the candle out and let her eyes adjust to the dark. At the window, she pulled the shutter back, wincing at the squeaky hinge, and peered out. The light of the half-moon illuminated the shadow of a figure just outside the gate. She saw sudden movement and then came another thud.

Who were these tormentors? And why did they not show their faces? Her throat tightened with anger at their secrecy.

Very publicly, the town had voted to dismiss her husband as minister in October. The news came as a great relief to her. It meant they could leave! They could return home to Connecticut, to her mother and father and her brother and his family. To the afternoons of tea and enlightened discussions about the Indian problem and fundraisers for the charity school. It meant rejoining a congregation of sympathetic neighbors who embraced her lovingly, who would be delighted to meet her boys. It would mean not worrying about petty slights from neighbors or whether her views on the Indian problem would upset the town leaders.

But Josiah wouldn't hear of their going home that soon. He had accounts and disputes to settle. If he left before the judge ruled in his defamation suit against Colonel North, how would that look? He couldn't let idle slander—Sabbath-breaking!—go unchallenged. He had his good name to clear!

What did it matter, she said, that slander had spoiled his good name in Hallowell? A small town upriver, not as far north as Winslow, but as far as anyone would want to travel. In Lebanon, there would be no need to even explain. Everyone would understand immediately. Didn't her own mother weep when they left, begging Josiah not to take her only daughter to such a savage wilderness? Hadn't her brother, Daniel, argued with Josiah about the unenlightened attitudes in such frontier places?

Josiah had thought he simply needed to part the Red Sea and his arrival would bring his people to enlightenment. "They will see, Sarah," he'd said to her. "The good people of Hallowell have only to hear about God's love and grace, and they will be led to understanding."

She had married him for his idealistic nature. Now that same quality appeared to her as stubborn naiveté. Even now, after all that had happened in Hallowell, he was away interviewing for a congregation in Dorchester.

In the front room, the fire had long gone out, and as she stood by the window, she could feel cold air come off the panes and through the floorboards.

The thudding had finally stopped, thank heaven. She hoped her tormentor had had enough for the night. She put her hand on the door to check that the board was securely in place. Her heart pounded such that she felt its pulsing in her throat. All it would take for an intruder to enter is a rock through a window pane. A persistent intruder could easily splinter the shutters.

She relit the candle and carried it to the table. She found a sheet of paper and her inkwell. For a moment, she hesitated, trying to find the right words, ones that conveyed her fear without unnecessary hysterics. *Trying circumstances? Unwelcome events? Worrisome intrusions?*

> Dear Josiah,
>
> Tonight someone, I do not know who, entered the front garden and hurled rocks onto the roof. This, after discovering a strangled hen on the doorstep in the morning. If the first had occurred without the latter, I might have dismissed it as a disgruntled neighbor who found the hen pecking in his garden. But stones? Fortunately, we do not live in a glass house. But I am concerned about these worrisome events. We need you at home. Adam and Isaac are well.
>
> Your loving wife,
> Sarah Brewster

She folded the letter, leaving it to be sealed in the morning, and went back to her bed, where the bed linens had chilled in her absence.

When she woke in the morning the boys' bed was empty but she could hear their nonsense patter in the next room.

In the kitchen, she found Isaac standing on a chair reaching for a bowl of bread covered in cloth. Adam hopped next to him, saying, "Aye! Aye!" as though encouraging a boat of men to row on course.

She swooped up Isaac in her arms. "What are you up to, you naughty boy?" She laughed and he threw his head back in glee while Adam called, "Mama! Mama!" and yanked at her night-dress.

"What will I do with such mischievous boys?" she said and kissed Isaac's chin and tugged at Adam's curls. "I imagine you want breakfast." Her own words alarmed her. What would she find outside the door today?

But she did not want to convey her fear to the boys. "Mama will get dressed and then I'll go hunting for eggs." Isaac wiggled with joy and Adam jumped up and down and then pulled her arm toward the bedroom.

Dressed, she took their hands and led them to the kitchen. "You sit here and eat your breakfast," she said, propping Isaac in his high seat and pulling the bowl of bread close to where Adam was climbing into a chair. She put butter on the table. "Adam," she said solemnly, pushing back the curls from his face. "You are in charge. Make sure your brother gets a tasty piece, do you hear?"

"Yes, Mama," he said, his attention already distracted by the bread and butter.

There was no time to waste. She turned and strode to the front door.

Outside, the day was a cold November gray. Her breath had quickened in anticipation and it made puffs of mist. The door-step was clear. She stepped out and looked at the spot where she had seen the figure the night before. Nothing. But all along the side of the house were stones, some the size of her fist. She picked one up, surprised at its weight. She imagined the shattering of glass such a stone could make.

She slipped the stone into her apron pocket. Inside the hen coop, the birds murmured and clucked, impatient to be freed.

She lifted the latch and watched the hens clamber across one another to be let out. They strutted about, pecking at the ground, confused not to find their food. "You are hungry, too, my dears," she said. She lifted the top of a barrel, reached in and scattered several handfuls of corn to the chickens. In the coop, she found nine warm eggs.

She cupped each egg in her palm and transferred it with care to her basket. As round and smooth as the stone, but lighter, their shells a delicate fortress easily breached.

When the Brewsters had first arrived in Hallowell, the people of the town welcomed them, if not exuberantly, at least with polite expectation. Mrs. North called and brought her squash seeds. The Lowry sisters, Martha and Grace, offered five chicks from their hens' recent broods. After the first Sunday's sermon, many of the townswomen clustered around her by the church entrance and congratulated her on her husband's post.

Colonel North and his wife came to call one afternoon a few months later and found Sarah serving tea to three Indian men as though they were refined guests. Jebediah Grasly, Moses Ablebody, and Seth Bard were all three graduates of the Indian school in Lebanon that Rev. Brewster had supported with money and ministering. On their way to mission work farther north, they had called in at the Brewsters. Sarah could see by the surprise in Colonel North's eyes that the last thing he expected to find in the Brewsters' parlor were Indians, even if they wore starched shirts and woolen trousers and sipped tea.

The Norths refused to sit or stay, but nodded tersely to Sarah before taking their leave. Of course, she had encountered such intolerance before—there had been many minds to convince about the charity school in Lebanon. But the alacrity with which the news spread in Hallowell and the almost complete and instant shunning that resulted shocked her.

Soon the butcher demanded full payment of their previous debt before honoring any more credit. Mrs. Almstead sent her oldest son to collect the sleigh Sarah had borrowed for her new weaving pattern. When Sarah brought her fabric to the dressmaker, Mrs. Hamlin insisted that the account be settled straight away. With Adam still crawling and Isaac on the way, Sarah had worried about their well-being in a town whose doors, if not yet closed, seemed to be closing.

Fortunately, Mrs. Bale, the midwife, cared not at all who the Brewsters hosted for tea. When Sarah grew sick near term with Isaac, Mrs. Bale sat with her during one long night, nursing her with simples to reduce her fever and encourage rest. Once Sarah's fever came down, Mrs. Bale, a tall woman with arms as strong as any man's, called in at least twice a day to check on Sarah's recovery. And when her childbirth pains came, Sarah could rely on Mrs. Bale's kind strength. But with no other female friends to help during her lying-in, Sarah had to hire Margaret Ferry, one of two free Negro women in Hallowell, to care for Adam.

Margaret was a reserved woman and Sarah failed to get much talk from her, though she knew Margaret could read—she had seen her in church with her hymn book—and the woman easily soothed Adam with her melodious humming. When Sarah's time came, Margaret was ready to assist the midwife, fetching water and handing her clean cloths, even letting Sarah grip her hand fiercely when the pain was crippling.

In her gratitude, Sarah named her second son after Margaret's husband, Isaac Ferry, though she could not tell if this pleased Margaret or not.

As Sarah boiled the eggs for her sons' breakfast, she made plans to post the letter to Josiah and to call on Mrs. Bale. Not sure if she could call the midwife a friend, Sarah hoped she could count on Mrs. Bale to provide her some assistance, or at the very least know whether these occurrences justified her alarm or were merely the pranks of mischievous boys.

She made herself strong tea to counter her exhaustion from her sleepless night. The tendrils of scented steam from her cup eased the strain she felt between her eyes.

Just then there came a sharp knock at the front door. Her shoulders tensed and she let out a startled "oh!"

"Who is it, Mama?" Adam asked, frowning, yellow crusts of yolk ringing his mouth. He had picked up on her worry.

She tried to calm her voice and appear unconcerned. "I do not know, my dear. But we shall soon found out!" She told the boys to stay where they were, and as she passed into the front room, she closed the door between it and the kitchen.

With her ear to the front door, she listened for the sound of the visitor. "Who is it?" she finally called loudly, and waited.

Silence. "Who calls?!" she said again, even louder, but there was no answer.

What did it mean? Who would knock in such a meaningful way and then not respond to her?

Sarah crept to the window and slowly opened the shutter a crack, angling her eye for a view of the front stoop. No one seemed to be there, unless he had flattened himself against the door in such a way that kept him from view.

"Who was it, Mama?" Adam asked when she returned to the kitchen table.

"Oh," she said, thinking quickly. "Only a sojourner passing through and asking to pick some of our winter kale."

At the port, Sarah found a boat whose captain was willing to deliver her letter down river. She thanked him and pressed two shillings into his hand to assure the letter's delivery.

Isaac was happy tied to her back in a sling. Adam had to stop and inspect every rock they passed and walk twice around every tree. Mrs. Bale's house was not far from the port but Sarah watched the sun climb higher in the sky and guessed that a quarter of an hour passed before they found themselves at the midwife's door.

Mrs. Bale's oldest daughter, Mehettable, answered the door. "I'm sorry," she said, "but my mother is attending a birth upriver."

"Will you please let her know I called?" Sarah asked, gripping Adam's hand so he wouldn't wander away.

"Of course," said Hitty. "Shall I tell her the reason for your visit?" The young woman glanced at the boys, already trained to look for signs of illness. A small child squealed from the back of the house.

Sarah hesitated. If it was only a social call, the midwife, always busy, might not return the visit for a few days. But there was no illness. "Only that I wanted to invite her for tea . . . when she is available," she added, to make it sound less demanding.

The younger woman nodded and shut the door, clearly eager to return to the sound of the squealing which had quickly turned into a wail.

Adam yanked on her arm when Sarah didn't move. "Mama! Let's go see the pretty sailboats again!"

"No, Adam!" she said too sharply. He stood, startled for a second, then his face crumpled and he cried. "I'm sorry, my dear," she said, stooping to his level. "I did not mean to sound so cross. We will buy some apples on our way home and make a pie."

Adam stopped crying to consider this offering. He sniffed and nodded, then peeled away and skipped across the slate stones to the road. In the yard stood the frost-blackened stalks of Mrs. Bale's herb garden soon to be buried in snow.

At home, Sarah rekindled the hot coals from breakfast and stoked a warming fire. She gave each of the boys one of the apples to gnaw on and set to peeling and slicing the rest. Fortunately, she had her own baking oven. How hard it would be to rely on neighbors' ovens to bake her breads and pies. And yet . . . perhaps such reliance might have occasioned more amity? As soon as she got the pie into the oven, she would write a letter to her mother to get her opinion on matters.

The afternoon passed without incident. She made a rich stew with the dead hen, which she had plucked and roasted the morning she found it, in part to give the boys the impression she had intended to kill it. They didn't know the hen had been one of her best layers.

She baked two loaves of bread along with the pie. While they were cooling, she gathered the boys and put their coats on. She had put off milking the she-goat as long as possible, and she wanted to do so before the sun set.

Adam watched her curiously as she peered out the front windows—it looked clear—and then led him, along with Isaac, to the back door. There were no windows on the back side of the house, which faced the north. Now she wished there were. No longer did settlers have to fear Indian attacks in New England, though news came of them from the west. There was only the winter's cold to fear. Until now.

She lifted Isaac and tied him to her back. If she had to run, she could carry Adam in her arms.

She set Adam behind the door jam, unbolted the door, and opened it a crack. If only the hinges didn't creak so!

No one was about. The fields behind the house stretched barren to the edge of the woods, the winter hay already gathered and baled.

Afraid to linger in the barn, she led the goat outside. Adam carried the pail. She set the stool down so that she could see both the house and barn at the same time, and set to work.

Adam turned in circles like a whirligig around her and the goat. Isaac giggled and flung his arms about her shoulders, which knocked her forward into the goat and some of the milk spattered to the ground. "Adam!" she said sternly. "Stop tickling your brother while Mama is working."

"Sorry, Mama," he said, laughing and running toward the goat. He reached out to tickle the goat which bleated with pleasure and flicked her ears for more.

"Sally likes it," she said and squeezed the goat's teat one last time. "There we go. Fresh milk for supper and cream for the morning."

As she stood up, she tensed, the hairs on her neck pricking up. She had been distracted by Adam's mischief and forgot for a few minutes about the fear that had stalked her all day. It was an odd, twilight sensation, this fleeting memory of a carefree moment that seemed already at such a great distance.

The sun was almost gone now and she hurried to put the goat back in the barn. With Adam toddling along in front, she carried the pail into the house. Once she checked all the shutters and bolts, they settled down for their supper.

The boys soon fell asleep, their bellies full of chicken and pie. Sarah set several heavy birch logs on the fire in hopes that it would burn for a while. She didn't plan to sleep, but she was so fatigued by the day that she didn't trust herself.

Sure enough, a few hours later, she woke in the rocking chair to the sound of someone banging on the front door. Her heart was in her throat. Her hand was in her apron pocket, curled around the stone she had picked up from the yard earlier. With her other hand, she gripped the poker she had laid across her lap before nodding off.

The fire had burned down to coals, thank the Lord.

The banging on the front door stopped. She watched the coals die down further and their light extinguish.

Then the banging started up again, this time at the back door.

Was it only one person? Or were others waiting for when she came out?

One ear listening for any sounds of waking from the boys, she stepped to the window and pulled the shutter open a crack. The clouds obscured the waning moon's glow and at first she could see only the dark outlines of the front fence.

The knocking continued on the back door, a furious pounding. It was possible that someone was trying to warn her of danger, or gather people to help with disaster, a fire in town, perhaps. But most people, if not everyone, would have known of her husband's absence. They would have either seen him leave early Friday morning or heard of his leaving in church on Sunday, which the Brewsters no longer attended, preferring now to observe the Sabbath at home. Neighbors, who kept a steady eye on comings and goings, would know he was still away because the horse was not out in the field.

The banging started up again on the front door while continuing at the back door. She gripped the poker, breathless, her stomach churning. So there were at least two of them! With one, she stood a chance. With two, or more, she would be overpowered.

Her eye at the shutter's opening, she strained to see who was at the front door. A dark figure came into view, but the shadows obscured any detail. It seemed the figure of a man, though, again, she saw only a dark lump and no outline of a head, which made it hard to determine whether it was man or woman.

She dared not call out to the figure, in case it woke the boys. But it was hard to believe they slept through the noise.

She tiptoed to the bedroom door and shut it so as not to make a sound. Then, at the front door again, she lifted her fist with the stone in it and knocked it against the wood planks.

The figure on the other side stopped banging, but the knocking from the back did not cease.

"Who are you?" she said in a loud whisper.

Silence from front and back.

"Who *are you?*" she said again, this time as loud as she dared.

She heard someone moving on the other side of the door, and then there was silence again. When she peered through the shutter crack, she no longer saw the shadows moving. She stood for what seemed hours, trying to hear the slightest sound from outside, but all was still.

In the morning, she woke in her bed. She had decided that it would be best to be in bed in the morning so as not to alarm the boys, but she had kept her day clothes on and slipped the poker under her pillow.

It was still dark. She rose to relight the fire. The night had been cold, probably the coldest one so far that season. Her fingers were stiff and she fumbled the logs, dropping one. She heard the boys stirring in the bedroom.

"Mama?" Adam called out, probably unwilling to leave the comfort of the warm bed linens.

"Yes, my dear!" she said, as brightly as she could. "I'm just starting the fire."

A thin layer of ice covered what was left of the goat milk. The ice easily cracked with a knife and she poured the thick, creamy milk into an iron pot over the fire. Soon, she had thick slices of yesterday's bread and warm goat's milk on the table.

In the bedroom, she found the boys, still sleepy, curled around each other. Leaning down and placing her cheek against Adam's, she whispered, "Time for lazy boys to rise." Little hands gripped her head and wrapped around her neck. She closed her eyes and sank into the smell of their sleep and the sweet caresses of their dimpled fingers. She gulped back a sob that rose in her without warning. She tickled the boys and was rewarded with shrieks that masked her crying and allowed her to wipe her wet eyes on the linens without their noticing.

When would Josiah return?

After breakfast, she opened the shutters to the meager light of dawn. The rooster crowed. She would need to open the coop—the coop! She had forgotten to round the hens up last night.

From inside, she didn't see anything or anyone in the front yard. Cautiously, while Adam and Isaac whacked each other with their socks in front of the fire, she opened the front door.

In the grip of frost, the ground did not reveal the footprints of her late night visitors. Had the terror of the night before been nothing but a dream?

Taken one by one, the events of the last two days could be explained away. A disgruntled neighbor warning her about her wandering chickens. Young boys playing a prank with stones. Someone come to call who had to leave suddenly. And, last night, the imagined terrors of a fatigued mind.

She wanted to believe these possibilities were true, but they did not conquer her fear.

And, yet—opening the door wide enough to pass across the threshold, she took in the morning: brightening with the rising sun, the sky looked clear; the last leaves had fallen and the frosted dew sparkled on tree branches; the air smelled of wood smoke and pine.

Inside, she scooped up Isaac and took Adam by the hand. "We have to round up the chickens," she told them. "It'll be a fun game, you'll see. Who can find the most hens?"

The boys squealed at the prospect, and Adam ran ahead toward the hen house. Atop the coop stood the rooster, his waddle jiggling as he peered down at Adam who poked his head into the coop. "Mama!" he yelled, and she ran toward him, hearing fright in his voice. His face appeared again. "Mama! The chickens are in their beds!"

"Oh!" she cried in relief. "How many?"

Adam looked back into the coop and then at the chubby fingers of his right hand. Unfurling each finger at a time, he counted up to five, declaring finally, "Five!" This number was invariably the answer to any question of how many since that was as far as he could count.

"Well, that's good," she said, ducking her head under the coop roof and counting the hens. There were six of them sitting on their beds, necks pulled in, roosting. A couple of hens opened one eye to look at her, then closed their eyes again and murmured to each other. "We only need to find five more."

With Adam leading the way, they looked around the hen house. They found one crouched under the house, one in front of the barn, and another sitting in the hayloft.

"Let's feed them," she said, "and maybe the others will come on their own."

She let Isaac reach into the barrel for a handful of corn and gave a mugful to Adam to scatter. The chickens they had already counted roused themselves, jumped down from their perches, came out from under the house, and pecked at the corn with pleasure. But no other hens came. Later, she would look farther afield to see if there were signs that a fox had taken advantage of her forgetfulness.

As they crossed the yard toward the house, she saw a horse coming down the street. She grabbed Adam and half carried, half pulled him to the house. "Mama!" he yelled.

"Be quiet, Adam!" she said, already regretful of her stern tone. She tried to soften her voice. "Let's see who this is, but go inside."

As the rider got closer, she sighed. It was a woman, thank heaven.

It was the midwife. Mrs. Bale stopped her horse at the gate and climbed down, then looped the reins around a fence post. "Good morning, Mrs. Brewster," she said.

"Good morning, Mrs. Bale," Sarah replied, never so happy to see the midwife.

"Mehettable said you called," the midwife explained, opening the gate, her ruddy cheeks even redder in the cold. "I'm sorry to come so early but I was just returning from Mr. Dawes's upriver—his wife had another girl—and I'm due to visit with Mrs. Trenway before noon. This was the only time I had to call."

"It's just fine," Sarah said. "Please do come in. I'll make tea."

"Oh! And I have a letter for you from Rev. Brewster. I stopped in for sugar at Mr. Owen's shop and he said it came early this morning and asked if I was traveling in this direction."

"Thank you!" Sarah took the folded square of paper and opened it immediately. But her heart sank when she saw the letter's date—Friday last. Of course there wouldn't have been time for her letter to arrive and his response to come so soon. She scanned her husband's words—he had delivered a well-received sermon the evening before and would be leaving on Monday after Sunday's service. Her letter would never reach him! It could take him anywhere from three days to a week to get home, depending on the weather and how long he stayed at the various towns along the way where he knew the pastors.

While Sarah heated the water over the fire, Mrs. Bale crouched down to say hello to Adam and Isaac. Adam knew her from when she nursed him during his bout of whooping cough in the spring.

"How are you, little Adam?" Mrs. Bale asked. "Are you taking care of your mother while Mr. Brewster is away?"

"Aye!" he said, grinning. He petted Isaac's hair while his little brother used Mrs. Bale's arm to pull himself to standing so he could gaze at her, a finger crooked over his lip.

"Such fine boys, Mrs. Brewster," the midwife said, gently cupping their heads in her hands. She took off her cap and cloak and set them on the sideboard. Isaac climbed up on a chair and she picked him up and sat down with him in her lap.

Sarah always admired the midwife's ease with children. Her manner was steady and forthright but always gentle. Not one to be left out, Adam climbed into Mrs. Bale's lap and she happily shifted Isaac to her other side to accommodate him, her strong arms encircling both boys.

Sarah busied herself with pouring the water into the teapot. Mrs. Bale's protective posture reminded her of her own vulnerable state. If it were only herself alone in the house to weather these odd events, she would not be half as fearful as she was.

As she poured the tea, she said, "I wish I could say that yesterday was merely a social call." She set a mug in front of Mrs. Bale and a small pitcher of milk. "But unfortunately there is something I want to ask you."

"Yes?" Mrs. Bale asked, her eyebrows raised.

"You know just about everyone in Hallowell, and, well, I wondered if you think there is anyone who might want to do us harm."

"Harm?" Mrs. Bale said, incredulously.

Sarah nodded. Her chest felt heavy. The worry and fatigue were weighing on her. "Yes, harm. You see, Mrs. Bale, there have been. . . ." She looked at the boys, then stood up and took Isaac from the midwife. "Come here, boys," she said, holding out her hand to Adam. "Why don't you play while Mrs. Bale and I talk?" She turned back to the kitchen and found a wooden bowl and two spoons. "Here you go. A drum. See?" She set Isaac down on a rug and showed him how to bang the bowl. It wouldn't keep them occupied for long, she knew, but she only needed a few minutes, and soon both boys were drumming the bowl with zeal.

At the table, she whispered to Mrs. Bale about the dead hen, the stones, and the insistent knocking.

The midwife listened attentively, her eyes sharp and unreadable. Sarah was unable to discern any reaction to what she said in the midwife's expression. When Sarah was done describing the events, the midwife sat silent.

"I know that . . . well, that it is not in your nature to talk . . ." Sarah hesitated, not knowing how to say what she wanted to say. The boys had now turned their attention from the wooden bowl and were paddling the rug and floorboards, busy with their noise-making.

The midwife cleared her throat and picked up her mug of tea. "No, I do not encourage idle talk."

"Oh, no, of course not!" Sarah quickly replied. "I do not ask you to gossip. I only wondered if you thought that I had cause to worry with the nature of these events."

Mrs. Bale smiled, her eyes softening, and reached for Sarah's hand across the table. "I can see that with Rev. Brewster away, you do worry. But I assure you that no one wishes you harm as far as I know. There have been some feelings about Rev. Brewster's suits, especially against Capt. North, but I cannot imagine that such people would want to harm *you*." She patted Sarah's hand and then drained her mug of tea. "No, there must be a simple explanation. As you mentioned, your hen most likely strayed into Mr. Warrington's or Mr. Bishop's garden. Mr. Bishop has been known to do worse to escaped pigs, taking them to the butcher for his own table. And there has been a rowdy crew in port these last two days, a boat waiting for a load of timber to take downriver."

"I hadn't heard about the boat and its crew," Sarah said.

"There. You see?" Mrs. Bale said, starting to gather her things. "You mustn't let these things worry you. You could mention the stone throwing to the constable. But I am sure Mr. Lowry will say the same thing as I do. He has had to jail a number of the men from that boat for public drunkenness."

Out of the corner of her eye, Sarah saw Adam wind his arm back in preparation to wallop his brother with the spoon. She rushed to him and grabbed the spoon away before it came down on Isaac who was trying to fit the large end of his spoon in his mouth so he could gum it.

"I do apologize for running," Mrs. Bale said, tying her wool cap under her chin. "Mrs. Trenway was in labor all night and I need to see how far along she is."

"Of course," Sarah said, smiling. "Babies do not wait for the midwife."

"No, they do not. It's rather the midwife who waits on the babies!" Mrs. Bale moved quickly toward the door and out. Sarah followed and watched the midwife unhitch her horse and mount. Within seconds, Mrs. Bale was gone. Sarah glanced up and down the road, then closed the door.

She cleaned up the tea dishes and sat down to knit while the boys experimented with the sounds they could coax out of a pewter bowl with spoons. While she worked and watched over the boys, in her head Sarah ran over the conversation with the midwife. Mrs. Bale was probably right. There were simple explanations for these events. She sighed, feeling reassured. It was a day in late November, the cold can fast bring fatigue, and the night comes early. It was easy for the imagination to get overworked.

For the rest of the day, she went about her work—washing the boys' underclothes, sweeping the rooms, cooking supper, milking the goat, shutting up the hen house—with a lighter heart than she had the last two days. What she needed was a good night's sleep. After putting the boys to bed with the story of Noah and the flood, she heated some water to bathe, luxuriating in the warmth of the water that cleansed her of the sour scent of her own fear. Clean and relaxed, she sat by the fire with her Bible. Her eyelids were soon heavy and sleep enveloped her.

Shattering glass woke her. Her body was stiff from cold and her position in the rocking chair. The fire had gone out.

Another explosion of breaking glass.

She fell forward to the floor and, feeling her way, crawled over glass and the wool rug to the bedroom door. They would have to kill her to get to the boys.

She reached up and closed the bedroom door, making sure it latched. The poker! She had forgotten to have it nearby her last night.

There was a muffled cry from the window, banging, the sound of men's voices.

She pulled herself up to standing. Heavy shoes thundered on the floor boards. "Who are you?" she said. "What do you want?"

In the darkness she could see only a mass of more darkness, something moving toward her, and then rough arms grabbing her, a hand over her mouth. She was dragged across the room, and through the door. They took her across the back yard and over the fence. She couldn't see their faces, but they spoke. "Not here!" one said. "There—there," the other said. She squeezed her eyes shut and prayed that the boys would not wake.

In their rough hands, she lost her sense of direction. She seemed to rise in the air but then the back of her head struck a rock.

She could not tell how long she had been unconscious. She

woke to the weight of a man on top of her, her hands pinned down, the pain of his rough thrusts inside her.

When she regained consciousness again, the first sound she understood was the crow of the rooster. There were other sounds—grunts? sneezing?—but they didn't make sense. There was a horrible stinging between her legs. Her neck ached. When she finally opened her eyes, she couldn't comprehend what she saw, what she felt. There was brightness and nothingness. Her tongue swollen and dry.

She sat up in a field, hay stalks cutting into her legs. A large sow was rooting in the dirt only a few feet from her, not even mildly interested in her presence. Her white nightdress was torn and dotted with what looked like blood. She nearly screamed, but caught herself and stood. Stumbling, ignoring the sharp stabs of hay on her feet, she ran to the fence and climbed over.

At the house, the door stood open, the broken window a dark hole. There was no sound coming from inside and she hesitated, afraid to enter. Her stomach lurched and she vomited.

Before she could think anymore, she propelled herself into the house. The bedroom door was still shut. As quietly as she could, she lifted the latch.

They were there! The boys were there! They sat in bed, Adam rocking Isaac gently and murmuring. They saw her and Adam yelled, "Mama! Mama!"

She held them tightly and buried her face into their sweet boy smell.

When Mr. Lowry, the constable, came, she did not know how to tell him about the attack. He saw the glass scattered on the floor of the front room and the broken window through which the cold blew in. He found the rocks that were used to shatter the window.

"Did you see who they were?" Mr. Lowry asked, peering at her over his spectacles. He was a heavy man who moved slowly and conveyed authority in his lack of superfluous movement.

"No," she said. "But I heard their voices."

"And recognized them?"

She looked over at Margaret Ferry, who sat with Adam and Isaac at the kitchen table. On her way back from summoning the constable, Sarah had stopped at the Ferrys to ask Margaret to help with the boys. As soon as she explained that there had been trouble at her house, Margaret put the bread dough she was kneading into a bowl and covered it with a damp linen. Without a word, Margaret banked her fire and put on her cloak. For once Sarah was grateful for Margaret's reticence in speaking.

"I'm not sure," she said to the constable.

"Had they been drinking?"

"I cannot say, though they did not seem unsteady in their movements."

"Movements?"

She glanced again at Margaret, who, seeing Sarah's look, ushered the boys into the bedroom.

Sarah sighed and looked at her hands. "They . . . well, they grabbed me."

"Did they do you harm?" the constable looked at her gravely. She nodded.

She could see that Mr. Lowry wanted her to say more but she could not bring herself to say what was so unspeakable.

"When is your husband to return?"

"Any day. Tomorrow, perhaps, at the earliest."

The constable nodded and then moved to the door. "You have somewhere to stay until then?"

"Yes," she answered, though she had no idea who would take her and the boys in.

"Good. Then, until Mr. Brewster returns," he said. With a quick nod, he put on his hat and lumbered out the door.

Margaret swept the glass into a pile and Isaac Ferry nailed a board over the window while Sarah made supper. They all ate in silence, even the boys, who glanced at the adults with anxious eyes. After dinner, she gave Isaac Ferry five shillings and nearly cried when Margaret whispered, "God bless you."

Her memory of the night before raked through her body, like a plough scraping the earth. As she sat before the fireplace, the boys fast asleep, she conjured the voices and faces of her attackers, Colonel North and his clerk, the young Edward Shalesworth. This knowledge grew slowly in her like heat, but once the memory woke all her senses, she felt as cold as the November air. Though she stoked the fire, she could not find relief and moved restlessly about the house trying to coax warmth into her frozen muscles.

Sarah was in bed, the boys huddled next to her, whimpering with hunger, when Margaret returned a couple days later.

The neighbor tried to rouse Sarah but she would not respond though her eyes were open. Margaret built up the fire and set water to heat. There was some frozen pie in the cupboard, which she heated by the fire and fed the boys with. She milked the bleating goat and gathered eggs from the hens.

When Margaret returned to the house with the goat's milk, Sarah was standing in the kitchen staring at the fire.

"Get the midwife," she said.

When Mrs. Bale came, she made a calming tea and a chamomile sachet that could be warmed and placed on Sarah's chest.

Alone with the midwife, Sarah said, "They came for me that night."

"Who?" the midwife asked absent-mindedly, accustomed to fevered patients.

"Mr. North and his man," Sarah said, watching intently for the midwife's reaction. "I know it was them."

Mrs. Bale stood still over her patient, her gaze seeming to assess Sarah's state.

Without a word, Mrs. Bale turned to her case and filled a ceramic jar with herbs and roots. She placed the jar on a high shelf. "If you need it," she said, without looking at Sarah. "Steep for five minutes and drink three times a day. It should have effect within three to four days."

Before she left, the midwife stood over Sarah's bed and said, "It's best not to stir more trouble."

Sarah closed her eyes. The midwife's horse trotted away. A cow lowed in a neighbor's yard. Margaret's voice murmured to the boys from the other side of the wall. The fire cracked and sparked.

She imagined Josiah's return. What would she say to him?

"Sarah," he might say. "Why did you not tell me?"

"How could I? The shame is unbearable as it is."

"But you are here, safe now," he would say, kissing her hand. His tenderness would make her cry more.

"Don't you see?" she would say, the anger gripping her chest. "It's because of you! Insisting on clearing your name."

He would let go of her hand, shaking his head. "Even if that were the reason, we can't let them frighten us away."

In the morning she would find the captain who took her letter, which her husband would never see. The captain could tell her when his boat would head downriver again. She would leave the animals in the care of Margaret and Isaac.

With her boys beside her on the boat, Hallowell would become a distant cove on the widening river.

She could already feel the soft give of her mother's front sofa, hear the clink of fine china teacups. She could see the glow of oil lamps and the well-worn leather of her mother's psalm book on the side table.

Geography Lesson

A siren wailed behind Pina. In the rearview mirror, a police cruiser maneuvered between the cars swarmed at the toll-booth. The cop stopped at one of the concrete barriers between the booths just ahead of Pina, next to a pot of marigolds. Fake nature. Summertime dusk was closing in and moths and other flying insects careened in the brightening flood lights.

She had somehow missed the sign for Exit 57 Monroeville, the one Evan, her very organized boyfriend, had told her to take. She had to exit at the next one, for Oakmont, wherever that was. The map Evan had printed out and highlighted for her was on the old Corolla's passenger seat next to a disheveled pile of his '80s rock CDs and an empty bag of popcorn. Evan had driven her to Hoboken to get her out of the city without mishap and caught the train back to their apartment. In the rush to leave, she had forgotten her charger.

She was headed to Pittsburgh. Papa had collapsed on the bus on the way home from work.

He was lucky, Mama had said on the phone, there were people around him. They helped him!

Mama seemed surprised that humans, ordinary people, would come to the aid of a stranger.

I'll never be able to thank them, Mama had said. I don't know who they are.

It was just like her mother to worry about thanking people while her husband lay in an induced coma.

How many of those bus passengers, aglow with witness status, were describing the story to their families and friends between bites of their supper?

There's no need to come now, Giuseppina, Mama had said, when you'd just have to wait.

Pina's hangover was only then lifting near the tail end of a sluggish workday, but how could she *not* go?

Well, if you want to, Mama said. But don't you have work? He wouldn't want you to miss work.

Work! If her parents, descendants of descendants of Italian immigrants, had any sense of the sacred, it was for work. Coal had collapsed, but the coke industry had kept going. Pittsburgh to Morgantown to Youngstown, then Pittsburgh again, wherever the company sent him. Nothing could interfere with work. For Pina, receptionist by day, bartender by night, work interfered with everything.

She imagined her mother at the kitchen table, fingernails bitten down to the quicks, the counters cleared of any sign of food and iced with a chalky film of Ajax. Her sisters were already there, Maria and Gina, always dutiful, the ones who didn't leave, married local guys, became bambini factories.

Where's your sense of direction? Maria, the oldest, liked to ask.

I've never had a sense of direction, she'd say, laughing off the criticism. It was true. Maybe metaphorically, but also literally.

How sweet it would be to call up a map of anywhere—the United States, Pittsburgh, Brooklyn—in her mind. To situate herself instantly in relation to the four cardinal points. An inner compass. She'd give her pinky fingers and toes to be able to climb out of any subway station and by instinct know which way to go, destination and route ingrained, like a migrating bird.

God knows Papa had tried to teach her, standing over an atlas at the table, but he was a geologist, not a teacher, and his intimate knowledge of the earth above ground and underground did not root in her.

Her phone had GPS, but she hadn't wanted to use up the battery and she was scared to rely on it. Sometimes it led her on a wild goose chase or spit her out the wrong way down one-way streets. In Italian: Senso Unico. Unique sense.

The cop got out of the cruiser and held his palms up, stopping anymore cars from advancing. She couldn't see what was happening but *something* was happening beyond the tollbooths.

Her bladder ached. She ejected the David Bowie CD. The exhaust of all the cars idling—the lucky ones with air conditioning—felt suffocating without any hint of a breeze.

There had to be a bathroom for the toll collectors, though actual live human collectors were becoming endangered species.

More sirens and lights, this time from the other side of the tollbooths. The low, keening note of an ambulance. Someone hurt. How awful, and yet she also couldn't help but feel aggravated because she was stuck. Is that how some of the bus passengers had felt when the stroke hit her father? Tired from work, school, just aching to be home, shoes off, dinner on the table. Maybe one or more riders anxious to relieve a home nurse aid, to soothe an aging parent, a sick spouse.

After her Papa was taken away by ambulance, what did the other bus passengers do? How awkward and silent the rest of their ride must have been.

What if she stood on top of her car and yelled, *My papa is dying and I have to pee!* But what made her situation more dire than anyone else's?

In the car behind her sat a man and woman, she assumed

married. A couple of kids bounced around to cheery music in the back. The woman's head was turned to the window, chin in hand, perhaps contemplating divorce. Or worse.

Pina's phone rang. As soon as she answered, her sister Gina's alto voice interrupted. Where are you?

Stuck at the exit. Is there news?

Listen. He—

The connection cut out. The phone battery light blinked red and then went dark. *He—what?*

The ambulance siren blared. Engines sputtered on around her. Brake lights winked in the night as cars stuttered forward.

A giant white eye swept across her car. The cop waving a flashlight to get her attention. Let's go! he ordered.

The cop directed cars to one side or another, the booths wide open, letting everyone pass through for free.

It was all a new world.

Keeping the Swans at Bay

Not only her stone face, laid back staring in the ferns,
But everything the scoop of the valley contains begins to move
(And beyond the horizon the trucks beat the highway.)

—Eiléan Ní Chuilleanáin, "Pygmalion's Image,"
The Magdalene Sermon and Earlier Poems

We were always at least one day ahead of my mother. By the time she arrived at the Stella Maris Holiday hostel in Galway, we had already secured a room in the Sligo youth hostel. There the river was home to a herd of swans that grazed the handouts from tourists. Peter and I went down the steep embankment to the river's edge with a bag of stale bread. The swans came on like the British fleet, confident in their mission. As I flung crumb after crumb out, increasingly more fearful that the swans, nearly as large as I was, would close in on us, we planned our next note.

"Dear Mom," I said. "We're sorry we missed you a second time . . ."

Peter grabbed a handful of bread crumbs and threw them far far out on the water so that the swans had to turn back and glide away from shore. "No, no, no," he said. "Dear Mom, Large swan fairies have spirited me away in the night. I've had to telegraph this message . . ."

"No one telegraphs anything anymore."

"They don't? That's a shame."

"How old are you?"

"Eighty-two. You know."

I jabbed him with my elbow.

"Dear Mom," he said. "I've fallen in love with a thirty-five-year-old Irish man and I've been in a terrible accident such that all vehicular motion except for the decrepit Irish bus system, dating back to the Viking era, gives me aneurysms. I'm stuck on this God-forsaken island for the rest of my life."

The swans took full advantage of the pause in crumb distribution to begin a full fleet attack, their dirty white bodies closing into the shore, and a few of them even wading towards us. They made strange grunting noises, as if they'd been crossbred with pigs, and stumbled awkwardly on land. I scattered the rest of the crumbs and we ran up the embankment.

"Dear Mom," I said. "There are only two things worth doing in life: Loving Peter and keeping the swans at bay."

Peter laughed into the wind and then kissed me.

I had been in Ireland two weeks when I met Peter at a ceili. He had spilled his stout on me and then offered to take me back to my hostel for a fresh change of clothes. I liked him a lot when he pinched the fabric of my t-shirt between his fingers and looked at me squarely to ask if it should be dry cleaned. I began to love him when with the same gentle seriousness he guided my legs apart before entering me.

My father had been against a gap year of travel in the first place for that very reason: I fell in love too quickly. I had fallen in love with a mechanic during one Florida vacation when we stopped for gas and I asked the man where the bathroom was.

What clinched it for me was the way he thoroughly wiped his hands of grease before even pointing in the direction of the restroom. He scrubbed his hands with Borox before lifting my skirt that night behind my parents' motel. When we left, I cried for days, refusing to eat, and my father threatened to call the police unless I ate. He had promised death to my high school history teacher and Mr. Donald then moved to a different district. They couldn't even take me to the circus, they said, because once they found me getting lessons on whip cracking from the lion tamer. My mother had reached the point where she wouldn't even let me look at the grocery store bagger, though he was almost the same age as I.

I never set out to fall in love. For my gap year I had other plans: to study my Irish heritage and "The Troubles," which still grabbed headlines back home. But best laid plans and all that. So when my mother called me in Dublin I knew that she was being sent over on a chaperoning mission. But she was too late.

That night my mother called our hostel.

"Claudia," she said. "Imagine my shock and surprise . . ."

"I know, Mom. We . . . I was just as surprised . . . How are you, Mom?"

"Tired. Exhausted. The bus ride was too long. I'm going to rent a car, I think."

"That wouldn't be such a great idea. You'd have to learn to drive on the other side of the road. Drivers here are crazy." I realized that in my desperation I was beginning to sound like her.

"Nonsense. I'll be there mid-morning tomorrow."

"Okay," I squeaked.

"Do you think you can last that long without . . . well, without doing anything rash?"

"Yes," I squawked and hung up. With her driving a car, it would be harder for Peter and me to stay ahead.

"Are you ashamed of me?" Peter asked, when I crawled into his bunk. "You don't want your mother to meet me, a washed-up old farmer."

"Agricultural engineer," I said. "You don't even own a farm."

"Even worse then."

I slid one hand under his shirt and around to his back, fingering the muscles that I watched rippling with movement when he biked ahead of me the week before the accident. I had followed him from rath to rath, visiting those prehistoric barns, large perfectly circular earth fortresses. He had a summer grant to visit farmers and see how they were treating the raths on their properties. This is why traveling by bike was important. Once at New Ross, waylaid for a couple days with a punctured tire, we were directed by the hostel owner to an unmapped rath. Trees had grown up in and around it so thickly that it looked like a mound until we were right on top of it. The mound was not a mound, but a ring that dipped inside like a huge bowl. As we ate bread and cheese, the farmer's sheep grazed around us. I sketched Peter napping in the sun at the other end of the rath, and a sheep eating very close to his head, maybe even nibbling a few of his hairs. When Peter woke he insisted that some of his hair was shorter on one side than the other.

My face so close to his our noses touched, I tousled his hair. "I'm not ashamed at all," I said. "I told you. My mother has incredible mind-controlling powers. She'll brainwash me into going back home with her. Anyway, she'll take one look at this," I touched the black and blue spot on my cheek, "and freak out."

We left the discussion at that, though I knew that Peter was unconvinced. But how could I explain that I wasn't ashamed of him, but of what he represented: my promiscuous passion. I was annoyed at my mother. Ireland was one thing I felt was mine that my mother couldn't touch. And I hadn't told her yet about the bike accident, knowing it would provoke the usual recrimination: Why weren't you wearing a helmet? You're lucky you didn't crack your head open. Why did you have to bike so far, anyway?

We had biked so far because the land told us to. That day of the accident, on the road at nine that morning we biked out of Dublin to Howth. By evening, the cool sweetness of the coming night intoxicated us. Pedal on, it said. And so we pedaled on. We were sailors hearing the Sirens. Then, just as I was turning a corner to a sudden expansive view of the ocean and sky and hills of green all at once, a small pooka of a stone wall popped out of the roadside. My wheel hit the wall and my bike and I orbited each other.

"*Claudia!*" Peter had screamed. After I woke up I remembered hearing his voice. But at the time there was no sound, there was a tunnel of silence that I had spiraled into, and there wasn't even feeling. Only seeing. And then darkness.

Peter flagged down a car—two men and a boy in the backseat—that took us to the hospital, but I couldn't recall much. There had been the warmth of Peter and his attention. The boy next to me who scrunched himself close to the door as if I were a leper. The man in the front passenger seat, older, drunk, who regaled us with tales of other gory bike accidents he witnessed and offered me beer and cigarettes to assuage my pain.

"T'ree of them once. One right after another, like a team of horses, over the cliff, down to the sea."

"Does it hurt?" Peter asked, touching my temple.

"A little."

"Dublin. Ohhh. Yes. You can be sure. They don't watch for cyclists. I've seen them, with my own eyes, coming broadside, catching the rear wheel. Tha's not how it happened to you, was it?"

"No," Peter shook his head. He looked out the window.

Afterwards, when I looked back on it, I thought the car ride was hysterical, and even Peter laughed about it, though he was the worse for wear having seen me fly and unable to do anything about it.

The hospital was dark and empty. It was Sunday, and I entertained the notion that hospitals in Ireland were closed on Sundays. The drunk old man helped me up the steps to the entrance. Peter followed behind with my backpack. The man led me inside and unsteadily guided me to a chair and then went to find a nurse. Peter, sweet Peter, his face grim, stood in front of me holding one of my bike pedals. And I laughed, a good laugh that filled me up and made my muscles, my spirits, everything, come alive again. Peter thought I was delirious.

And maybe I was. The hospital doctor wanted me to stay overnight to be sure there was no concussion, but I refused. There were no broken bones, only a bruise where my head made contact with the road and an occasional throbbing in my temple. And I had lost my usual relation to space.

If I looked down while walking, the ground rushed at me. When I stepped out into the street, cars picked up speed and barreled down on me. In Dublin, the snot-green double-deckers were the worst. Peter always insisted on sitting on top at the very front where I was sure that streetlamps were going to shave off the windshield. Everything was close in this city, streets were narrow, shops huddled together. Even on O'Connell Street, the widest boulevard in Europe according to the guidebook, the people jostled elbow to elbow on the sidewalks.

I tried to draw but proportions came out strange. Distances were indistinguishable, eyes melted into noses, hands grew larger than heads.

After Sligo, we made five bus changes to get to the tip of Crohy Head in Donegal. We had left a note in Sligo. "Dear Mom, Hope you enjoyed the beautiful bogland and blue mountains of Connemara. I've decided to push on to Donegal. Hope to see you there at the Crohy Head hostel."

We got in late and found a message from my mom: "Dear Claudia, I'm at the Ram's Head Inn in Carrick. The Connemara was lovely but brief."

I liked this new method of communicating. Maybe if we finally met up we could just pass postcards back and forth to each other.

Dear Mom, Holding off on college for now. Maybe some art courses. Isn't it a nice day out?

Dear Claudia, You do that. We understand perfectly. Dinner will be ready soon.

She was only a couple hours away.

Peter was beginning to get anxious. "We can't just keep circling the island. I have work to do."

"Just a few more days. Until my bruise goes away."

We got up at five the next morning and started hitchhiking. A man wearing a business suit picked us up in a gray Renault. It was the first time I had been in a car since the accident. The car moved faster than any bus and was so low to the ground I was sure it was going to slip under the wheels of oncoming trucks. We had only been driving for ten minutes when the acid in my stomach rose up the back of my throat. My right leg muscles cramped from pressing down on an imaginary brake. I was trying not to look out the front windshield, but as the car weaved into the right lane to pass, my eyes ached from trying to grip the road racing under us.

"Could we just pull off for a minute?"

The man glanced over at me, then back to the road. "Why? What's wrong?"

"I guess I'm just not used to being in a car. I think I'm going to puke."

The man pulled the car over to the side of the road and said, "Stop taking the drugs, missy."

My knees shook when I got out of the car. I held on to the door handle, taking big gulps of air, the ground underneath me swaying.

"She's not taking drugs," Peter said. "She's been in a bike accident." Peter leaned forward from the back. "Are you going to be okay?"

I looked at the road ahead of us and could still feel the car zooming along freely like it might suddenly swerve into the trees. "I can't get back in the car."

"I'm due in Belfast at nine," the driver said.

"Okay. Okay." Peter got out and pulled our packs from the back seat. "Cheers," he said and closed the door.

"Now listen," he said. "We're going to stop this ridiculous crusade that you've talked me into. Here's what we do. We'll walk back to that shop we passed two minutes ago and get you to hospital."

"Don't get mad."

"Mad? Mad? Why do Americans always use that word? Mad means you're frothing at the mouth with insanity. Do you understand? The word is *angry*. Angry! And I'm not angry!"

"Yes, you are. You're full of wrath."

He sighed and slung the backpacks together over his shoulder. "I'm *not* full of wrath. Though I should be looking for one."

"That's why walking is so good." And I marched along, happy that the ground wasn't moving. The worst that could happen was that I might trip over a snail.

When we got to the shop, which was a butcher's at the side of the road, alone in its commerce, surrounded only by tall whips of grass, Peter wanted to call an ambulance. But the butcher shop was closed.

"Maybe," I said, "If I sat in the back seat it wouldn't be as bad.

In the front seat I feel as though I'm going to tip out the front window and everything is coming at me like a train."

Within five minutes a car stopped. An old farmer from the looks of him, but he was only going a few miles before turning off. Then a few minutes later, another car pulled over. Two women. Peter and I slid into the back. "Thanks for stopping," I said. "How far are you going?"

"You're American, are you?" The older woman, who was driving, twisted around in her seat to look at me.

"Yes, I am. He's not."

She looked at Peter and smiled. The younger woman, who had the same brown eyes and freckles, smiled at us, too. They both had dark brown hair and ruddy faces and wore black dresses.

"Close to the border," the young woman said. "We're going to a funeral."

"Oh, good!" I said. Then, "I mean, good for us that you're going that far, not that you're going to a funeral."

The older woman laughed and pulled back out onto the road.

"It's only a distant great uncle," the younger one said.

"Listen to you! Only. Only!" The mother's voice was cut with sudden impatience, as if they were resuming an earlier conversation.

"Well, it's true," the daughter whined, and I realized she was in her teens. It was difficult to pinpoint her age. "I've only met him twice before," she said and looked back at me as though I could sympathize.

But I was too busy concentrating on motion to sympathize. The back seat was better, though not by much. The car jerked from side to side whenever the mother changed gears. I submitted to the assault of trees whipping by, not daring to look at the speedometer which I could have easily seen by turning my head. There were too many trees to count, and soon they gave way to open land. At first, by concentrating on the imagined feel of the car on the soft earth, my stomach calmed down. Then, suddenly, the road charged at us and the sky and sea tumbled around me, the same view from the air as when I had flipped over my bike. My body jerked and my stomach dropped into my bowels. I opened my eyes and studied the brown vinyl of the driver's seat in front of me. It had a craggy surface like the skin of a turtle.

Peter's hand covered mine. His lips came close to my ear. "Are you all right?"

His low, warm voice reminded me of that first moment when I came out of the black. He was saying my name, begging me to wake up. And I had been a giant eye. The sky and grassy embankment were the first things I saw, but I couldn't see myself. I kept trying to look down at my hands, but the sky and earth and Peter's face were the only things that swung back and forth in front of me.

"Can you feel your body?" he had asked.

I had to think about it a few minutes. Did I have a body? I couldn't see it, but I felt a weight underneath my eyes, and then I concentrated and felt the cold gritty surface of the road underneath me. And my hands, scraped open, began to burn. Later at the hospital, I thought again about that question. It had been more than an inquiry about my health, it had been an invocation, calling forth my body. And later, after the soreness was gone, I still couldn't always connect the sensations of my limbs to myself. When Peter gripped my thighs as I sprawled on top of him, his hands steadied me more than they thrilled me, and I tumbled away from the rocking of our bodies.

We swerved abruptly to the right. We were passing a tractor. The car shuddered as it picked up speed, and then I saw that there was another car coming directly at us.

"Drop back!" I screamed. The oncoming car was approaching at a phenomenal speed. The woman pressed on the gas pedal.

The other car was only a few hundred feet ahead, then fifty, then twenty, then it was smashing into us over and over. I covered my face with my hands, like a small child at a horror movie. Our car swerved left, and shortly after there was a loud *whoosh*. We were back in our lane and the tractor was a green insect crawling along the edge of the landscape.

No one else in the car had even blinked, and I burned with embarrassment over my outburst. The mother and daughter were still squabbling over their relative.

"You've seen him more than twice," the mother said.

"No. He's seen me. But I was too young to remember."

"Anyway, there'll be loads of family there."

"Except Da. Because he's too busy," the daughter sing-songed.

The mother's hand flashed out from the steering wheel and smacked her daughter's leg.

"Ouch!" the daughter shrieked and rubbed her knee. I looked down at Peter's hand covering mine. For the past three days, no one had asked about the bruise on my cheek, had maybe not even noticed it. Or noticed it, but not thought anything strange about it.

They dropped us off just before the border at the side of the road. They had gone a ways beyond their turnoff, so their car did a U-turn in the road and we waved at them as they retreated the way we had come. Ahead of us, toward Derry, a gray, metal tower, like the ones atop submarines, rose up from the middle of the road.

"I'm ready for a nibble," Peter said and bit my ear.

We sat on top of a fence by the side of the road and ate cheese and crackers and apples, watching the tower watching us.

"Let's wait for her in Derry," he said.

I opened up the guidebook. "The 'Provisional' faction of the IRA, which has dominated the fractured networks of militant republicanism since December 1969, adroitly exploited military insensitivity in order to redirect Catholics' indignation from their

Protestant neighbors towards Britain and its 'army of occupation.' Anglophobia was intensified after 'Bloody Sunday' when thirteen people were killed by soldiers in Derry. As the security forces rendered themselves less vulnerable and eventually less obnoxious, terrorism was readdressed to sectarian and factional targets, which accounted for the majority of killings in 1975."

"What a bunch of shite! Nothing like a balanced sense of history. Anglophobia. Really. Let me see that book."

"No, wait." I opened to another page and pointed to a heading in bold: "CARRICK-A-REDE. As you draw even with Carrick-a-Rede island, you'll see the rope bridge, the second biggest tourist attraction in these parts. Strung eighty feet above the sea, between the mainland and the island, the bridge leads to a commercial salmon fishery on the southeast of Carrick-a-Rede—but its main function is to scare tourists, something it does very successfully. Walking its sixty-foot length, as the bridge leaps and bucks under you, is enough to induce giggles and screams from the hardiest of people."

"Claudia. I think we should stop in Derry and you should see a doctor. I don't think they did a very thorough examination at the hospital. If you're still feeling dizzy . . ."

"If I go to a doctor in Derry, can we go to this place?" I pointed at the guidebook.

"Okay," he sighed. "What a fool you're making of me."

We walked down the road towards the tower where soldiers stood with binoculars and guns. They didn't ask us to stop but their eyes followed us all the way past. An hour later we were signed in at the Derry hostel where everything was new and clean, the sheets like they'd never been slept on before. I lay down on a bottom bunk while Peter put his stuff away in a men's dorm across the hall. The bunk was made out of recently varnished pine that smelled heavenly.

When we went down to the lobby to get a map of the city, the guy behind the counter said, "You're Claudia Gibson, eh? You just checked in?"

"Yes."

"Someone just rang for you and left a message." He pushed a sheet of paper across the counter. It said: "Dear Claudia, I finally found you. Your note at Crohy Head didn't say where you'd be. I called everywhere. I'm in Letterkenny now. Will be in Derry soon. Wait for me."

"Peter," I said. "She's coming."

"Good. I can't wait to see her. I'm beginning to think she has three heads. Or maybe I have three heads."

"You don't understand."

"I think I do," he said and cupped my cheek in his hand. I let his hand take the weight of my head, then I winced as a sharp pain shot up to my temple.

"What is it?"

"Nothing. Just a headache. I want to lie down."

The next morning, I woke early, while it was still dark out, dressed and checked out. There were buses leaving for the Causeway Coast in front of a travel agency down the street. I tried not to think of Peter's face, slack with sleep against his pillow, as the bus pulled away from the curb and wound around the narrow streets. The sun rose pink and yellow, giving a silver shine to barbed wire. Through an alley way I caught a glimpse of a tank and the young faces of scared men. I knew then that it would all catch up to me eventually, but I wanted to wait a little longer. So, I gave into the soothing, steady rumble of the bus engine.

When I woke, my neck was stiff and the bus was climbing a hill along the coast. I felt like I was riding a whale on a mountain. We went higher and higher above the sea toward the sun. An hour or so later, the bus driver let me off at the side of the road, in what looked like the middle of nowhere.

"Another bus in an hour," he said, and the doors hissed shut.

There was a white-washed sign nearby that said in shiny black letters: Carrick-a-Rede, 2 km. and an arrow that pointed toward a narrow, one-car road. The road eventually ended in a small, empty parking lot and beyond it a dirt path cut through the high grass along the cliff edge. I stumbled along, my tongue thick from thirst, my head pounding. I thought I was hearing things as I approached the end of the path where it dropped down to steep wooden stairs. Voices swam about in the wind. The stairs were big blocks of wood embedded in the red clay of the cliff. The rope bridge, creaking and straining against itself, dipped out over swirling white caps of water. I gripped the rope railing and stepped onto the wood planks. I looked up and across at the waving grass on the other side of the bridge. The boulder spun around and around, so I looked away quickly, down at the planks of wood again. If I just concentrated on them, everything would be fine. I stepped out farther. Farther and farther. I went faster, intoxicated by the rhythm of my feet on the wood.

"Claudia!"

I stopped and that's when I felt the swing and rock of the bridge. Then I saw the water sloshing below. I didn't want to look up. I closed my eyes and held on to the ropes on either side and slowly turned around, then opened my eyes.

Peter and my mother were standing on the stairs, their hands cupped to their mouths, their words rushing into the wind.

"Dear Mom!" I shouted. "I can't help myself. I can't help it. I love him and there's nothing to do about it! I fell off my bike onto my head. But it's my fault. Mine! My fault! Not yours!"

"Look!" Peter pointed out toward the sea.

At first there was nothing to see, the sleepy roll of the current, a white crest here and there, a cormorant diving. And then, almost too quickly to believe, the black curve of a dolphin's back slipped like an onyx button through the water's surface. Another one. Three all at once. The wind threw itself against me. The cold passed through my bones, as though I wasn't made of solid matter, but of cheesecloth. I stayed there, swinging with the bridge, and the world didn't move. Only I did. Then the dolphins slipped into the vast darkness of the ocean, and the horizon became a long, steady line against the sky.

Acknowledgments

I am grateful to Laurel Thatcher Ulrich's *A Midwife's Tale: The Life of Martha Ballard Based on Her Diary, 1785–1812*, where I first encountered references to Sarah Brewster.

These stories were written over the course of a couple decades and with the help and encouragement of many people. I am, of course, indebted to Hidden River Arts and its mission of support for underserved writers and artists. I am forever thankful for my mentors along the way: Jim Daniels, Sharon Dilworth, Laurie Doyle, Noy Holland, Hilary Masters, Reginald McKnight, Jay Neugeboren, Peggy O'Brien, Ron Welburn, and John Edgar Wideman. Thank you to the Pittsburgh Ladies—Julie Albright, Jen Bannan, Erika Gentry, and Lorraine Miller—especially for all the love and laughter. I cannot thank the Fiction Babes enough: Thérèse Soukar Chehade, Tamara Grogan, Lesley Hyatt, Nicole Nemec, Elizabeth Porto, Kamila Shamsie, Pam Thompson, and, of course, honorary babe Herman Fong, and in a later configuration, Becky Lartigue and Anna Smith. I am also grateful to Dennis Gildea, Rick Paar, and Kyle Palazzi, who met some of these stories in draft form and were kind to them. *Gros bisous* to Claire Boulanger and the whole Boulanger *famille*. My love for writing started with a love for reading, fostered by my first teachers, Rosetta and Kenneth Dymond. Finally, it is impossible for me to fully express my gratitude to Louis Faassen, for all the love, cooking, art, and companionship throughout the years represented by this collection.

CPSIA information can be obtained
at www.ICGtesting.com
Printed in the USA
BVHW030305300721
613243BV00006B/189